Grizzly Cove

Spirit Bear

BIANCA D'ARC

She never thought she would love again...and then he appeared in her life.

Rescued alive, but not whole...

Laura is a white wolf shifter far from home and out of her element. She's been held prisoner for years by those who would use her power for their evil purposes, but she's held strong against them and lived to tell the tale. But she's lost everything in the process—her mate, her baby girl, her zeal for living. Her baby is a grown woman now, and Laura is overjoyed to be reunited with her only child, but questions remain.

Is he her friend, or warden?

Tasked by the Alpha of his Clan to watch over Laura's recovery, Gus feels especially drawn to the injured woman. He is a rare spirit bear shifter who walks the shaman's path. Considered spooky by most of his friends, Gus finds acceptance and welcome from Laura that he cannot resist. The question bothers him - and his Alpha - was her escape too easy? Has she been delivered into their midst as some kind of living Trojan Horse?

How can he be her true mate?

Laura begins to realize that the so-called mate she'd had years ago may not have been her one, true mate. Her attraction to Gus is too strong to be denied and she feels things for him that she never felt with her baby's father. New feelings are stirring - as is a feeling of danger and inexplicable rage when she sees anybody other than Gus or her daughter. Something is wrong. Very wrong. She will need help to defeat the residual evil left on her by years of captivity. She only hopes Gus and the good people of Grizzly Cove will be up to the task - and that something will be left after the evil is washed away. She's only just regained her life. She doesn't want to lose it again...this time, possibly, forever.

DEDICATION

To my Dad, who is feeling a bit under the weather as I finalize this book, but will hopefully be back to his fighting form soon. He turns 94 in a few weeks and they just don't build 'em like him anymore. It really is true – the WWII generation really was "the greatest generation." At least, if my dear ol' Dad is anything to go by!

Special thanks to Vanessa Ramirez and Marissa Va for being such dedicated supporters and longtime readers. I'm so happy to have gotten to know you both a bit, and I hope you both enjoy this book very much!

And many thanks to my editor, Jessica Bimberg, and my dear friend, Peggy McChesney, both of whom helped to catch my mistakes and make this book better. Love you gals!

PROLOGUE

Big John had a problem. Since convincing his former Spec Ops unit to settle in one place and start a new town on a wilder part of the Washington coastline, things had gone a bit out of control. The town was coming along nicely, and more people—shifters, mostly—were coming in to settle here, as he'd hoped would happen. But Grizzly Cove was still very much an experiment. A *what if?*

Like, *what if* a group of normally solitary bear shifters all settled in one place and worked together to make a home for themselves? His team had been all over the globe, fighting evil on behalf of Uncle Sam, and they'd enjoyed their time in service, but now, it was time to settle down and start families—if only they could find their mates.

The band of brothers that had served together was the basis for the town. John had put out the word on the shifter grapevine that female bear shifters were welcome to come to Grizzly Cove and look over the men there—all bear shifters in the core group—and see if maybe one of them was their mate. A few had come, but unexpectedly, even more Others had arrived.

They'd been checked out by the Master vampire of Seattle—a truly ancient guy named Hiram—who wanted to know what their intentions were. They'd managed to form an alliance that had, so far, served both parties well, and there had been visitations from quite a few Others, as well.

For instance, John hadn't counted on the pod of merpeople seeking refuge in the cove waters and in the rapidly expanding town center. He also hadn't counted on the mages, most notably, the *strega* sisters, one of whom was now his mate. Their *nonna* had joined them here, and now there was an actively growing magic circle that got together when needed. John shook his head. For all his strategic planning, he could never have envisioned that.

Evil had come to call, too. First, the leviathan and its ugly minions had menaced them from the water. The mages had been key in pushing that monster back into the deep, but it was still out there, just waiting for someone to be foolish enough to go out past the new protections, into the open waters of the ocean. It fed on magical energy, and apparently, the concentration of highly-magical bear shifters in the town had attracted it.

Then, agents of the *Venifucus*—an ancient order dedicated to world domination through their banished leader, Elspeth, known as the Destroyer of Worlds—had repeatedly tried to infiltrate the town. John's mate, Urse, had used her truly awesome magic to put up permanent wards around the town that would not allow evil to pass through. That stopped the threats from entering the territory, but just in the past few weeks, two separate women had been chased all the way to Grizzly Cove, and massive showdowns had happened just at the border.

So much for keeping a low profile.

And now, one of the recent arrivals had brought a new sort of magical threat into town. Imprisoned by several different *Venifucus* mages for decades, Laura Stanhope was finally free. She seemed nice enough, and she was the long-lost mother of Marilee, the woman who'd been chased into town and found a bear shifter mate all her own, but John still wasn't entirely sure Laura could be trusted.

Oh, he didn't think Laura would consciously try to harm

anyone in Grizzly Cove, but she'd been held against her will for so very long. By mages. Who knew what they'd done to her? She could be some kind of sleeper agent, or a Trojan horse designed to penetrate the ward and then wreak havoc from inside the town. John wasn't sure, and he didn't like not having enough data to make a plan.

Which was why he had cornered one of his most trusted men and former soldiers, Gus.

"I want you to keep an eye on Laura," John said without preamble. It wasn't his way to prevaricate.

"You don't seriously think she could give us any trouble?" Gus was a shaman and, perhaps, a bit too trusting at times because of his spiritual path, but he was a trustworthy soul, and John knew he was the right man for this job.

"The Trojans had a horse. Al-Qaeda used sleeper cells. She made it past the ward, but that could be because she, herself, is okay. But she was held prisoner for a long time. Who knows what was done to her?" John frowned. He hated thinking about the treatment that poor woman had received at the hands of their enemies, but he had to think of the rest of his people, as well. "Just keep an eye out. That's all. I'm not saying she's a plant, but I have to think about the big picture."

Gus was frowning too. "I see what you mean, but I don't like it."

"I don't like it either, but it's my job to consider all possibilities, and right now, Laura is a big question mark in my mind," John admitted. "I need more data, and I don't want to do it the old-fashioned way by interrogating the poor woman. She's been through enough. We have to be more subtle."

"So, you want me to spy on her." It wasn't a question, but John knew Gus understood how vital it was to keep their brothers-in-arms and the women and Others who had come here to live among them safe.

Protecting others was at the very core of their beings. None of the original group would countenance a threat to the peace and stability of the town. It was just beyond imagining.

"Observe and report any problems, yes," John confirmed.

"Why me?" Gus asked, then went on to answer his own question. "I suppose it's because of my magical background and chosen path as a shaman."

"That, and you seem to have developed a friendship with the lady. I thought it would be easier on her to have someone she knows, and appears to like, checking on her than one of the other guys," John admitted.

Gus shook his head. "If she finds out I'm a spy, she's going to be more hurt because we're friends. Did you think of that?"

John regarded Gus steadily. "So, don't let her find out. You used to be good at subterfuge before you went all squirrely on us."

"You mean before I found my calling?" Gus shook his head. "John, sometimes it takes a while on the wrong side of things to show you what's really important. I was, perhaps, too good at lying to get what I wanted in the old days. I've changed my ways, for the better."

"Less convenient to me," John stated baldly. "Especially right now, in this situation. And you never lied to any of us on the team. You only prevaricated when it was for the good of our missions. You weren't a liar. You were an operative. There's a difference."

"Semantics, boss," Gus disagreed, but without heat.

John knew Gus's conscience had come out in a big way since he'd started training as a shaman soon after they'd all retired. He'd achieved a lot in a comparatively short time and had been granted leave by his teachers in other parts of the country to come back and work among his Clan, following his chosen path. Gus also ministered to the nearby Native American population, helping the local tribe when they needed a hand.

John admired Gus's vocation, even though it was proving to be a little inconvenient at the moment. Still, he knew he could count on Gus to act for the good of everyone in

Grizzly Cove. He wouldn't let them down. He just had to work his way around to accepting the mission. John watched patiently. He knew Gus was thinking over all the angles and would soon come to the undeniably correct conclusion.

"Well, think about it, and let me know what you decide," John said after a moment.

He couldn't order Gus to do anything. They weren't in the military anymore, and even back then, unless it was a battlefield situation where his men had to follow orders without question, he usually had to coax them into his way of thinking about an op beforehand. They were bear shifters, after all. Independent thinkers. Three hundred pounds of animal instinct with razor sharp claws and lightning reflexes. Solitary, usually.

Having them all together in one unit of operatives had taken some getting used to, but once they'd accepted John as Alpha—though that meant something a little different to bears than it did to Pack animals, like wolves—they'd become one of the best units Uncle Sam's military had ever produced. Phenomenal success rate. Near-perfect record. A well-oiled machine.

They were finding success as civilians, as well. The crazy plan to camouflage their new town as an artists' colony had been thought insane at first, but was actually working quite well. They'd set the place up as a closed community, where anybody who wanted to live in the town had to apply for acceptance. The town council was made up of the members of the old unit, and they examined every application of those who wanted to move here and start businesses or actually be artists.

So far, they'd accepted three human sisters who had opened a fantastic bakery, two other sisters who had opened a book shop and had turned out to be witches. All five of those ladies had mated with one of the original group of single bear shifters and made them the happiest of men. John counted that a success, all the way around. His men were finding their true mates and were able to settle down and make a home. There were other matings—most recently a werewolf and a new bear that they'd welcomed into town—Marilee and King. It was Marilee's mother who was the current problem and potential security threat.

Gus was still single. He'd already befriended Laura, Marilee's mother. He was the perfect person to keep an eye on things with as little fuss as possible. He'd come around sooner or later and realize what he had to do. John made to leave, but Gus's words stopped him.

"What if she is a threat? Do we just eliminate her?" Gus's tone was both angry and bleak.

John shook his head. "That would be the easiest way, of course." John didn't lie to his people, and he wasn't about to start now. "But, she's Marilee's mother. Laura has been through hell, and she has important intel on all those *Venifucus* mages and hangers-on who tortured and imprisoned her for all those years. We need to know what she can tell us, and personally, I want to be able to clear her so that Marilee can finally have her mother back. The biggest problem is knowing whether or not she is a real threat to the town." John sighed. "Eliminating her would be the last resort. I want to see her live a full and happy life, if at all possible."

Gus held his gaze for a long moment, then nodded. "Good. I want that too."

CHAPTER 1

Laura was enjoying getting to know her only child, her daughter, Marilee. Laura had been forced to give up her baby while running from evil *Venifucus* agents who, eventually, had caught her and imprisoned her for over twenty years. She'd managed to place little Lee Lee, as she called Marilee back then, with what she thought was a strong werewolf Pack in the wilds of the Canadian Rockies, but she had come to learn that, while the Pack and it's Alpha, Tobias, had protected Marilee, they hadn't really welcomed her.

Marilee had grown up as an outsider. Some of that was to be expected, of course. Marilee and her mother were white Arctic wolves, and the Canadian wolves had been timber wolves of mostly gray and brown. In addition, Laura and her daughter were touched by a great deal of magic. More magic than the average werewolf.

Laura had an ancestor who had been born of the fey realm. More than that, Laura had mated with a human mage, so Marilee had a legacy of even more magic than Laura herself had ever had. Magic on both sides. Some of this mortal realm, and some from…elsewhere. Add that to the sparkly white fur, and Marilee had been born to stand out.

The timber wolves of Tobias's Pack hadn't liked that. They'd hidden themselves away up north, in a remote mountain valley that wasn't easy to find. They had chosen to hide rather than deal with the trouble they all sensed was coming. That Tobias had agreed to take on Marilee at all was remarkable, in retrospect, but perhaps, he did have a heart, after all. He might have been a good Alpha at one time, but that appeared to no longer be the case.

If Tobias had been the kind of man—the kind of leader—Laura had thought he was, her daughter would not have been so marginalized under his leadership. She wouldn't now be such a timid little thing, though she was definitely starting to come out of her shell since mating with King. He had a strong, dominant personality, but he used his strength to bolster Marilee's sometimes shaky confidence in herself. He never tried to dominate Marilee in a bad way. He gave her room to grow, and Laura couldn't be happier with the way things had turned out for them both.

As for her own plight, Laura just wasn't certain about anything, anymore. She was free for the first time in decades, which was magnificent, but it had been so long since she had been free to do as she wished with her life, she really didn't know where to start. The people of Grizzly Cove had been wonderfully supportive. They'd given her time, and breathing space, to try to figure out what she was going to do, but she knew, sooner or later, she would have to find some way to support herself. She had no money. No identification, even. She was essentially a non-person in the eyes of human law. She'd been out of circulation for a very long time.

Even if she wanted to leave Grizzly Cove, she no longer had the kind of paperwork people generally did in this, the information age. Big John, the Alpha of the bear Clan that had started the town, had asked one of his people to gather some preliminary documentation for her, only to find that she had been declared legally deceased long ago. Her home Pack had disappeared, though they had always lived in a remote area that was sparsely inhabited, and seldom traveled. They were probably all right, just keeping a low profile.

But it was very inconvenient for Laura. She had no

documentation. No birth certificate or legal standing. In the eyes of the human world and their laws, she didn't exist.

So, how could she leave Grizzly Cove looking for work? She was undocumented. She could take her chances as an undocumented person—or *illegal alien*, as it had been called in her day—but there were further complications. The most important being, that she was still being hunted by the *Venifucus*. Now that she was awake—out of the self-imposed coma state she had used to deny her captors any more of her power—she was a very valuable commodity to those who had imprisoned her for so long.

There was no way in hell she was ever going back to that. She would sooner die than be chained again, and she'd vowed to herself that she would take a few of them with her if that was to be her fate. Laura had a lot of anger and rage bottled up from her years of confinement. Her inner wolf was ready—no, *eager*—to kill those who had kept her prisoner for so long.

But these were thoughts for another day. Today, she was meeting Marilee for lunch at the picnic tables down by the water, in the heart of town. Marilee had said she would stop by the bakery and pick up sandwiches for them both, then meet Laura at what had become her favorite spot—the picnic table she had first walked to when she was finally able to stand on her own and walk out the back door of the clinic, which wasn't too far away.

She'd been in rough shape when she had been brought to town. She had been unconscious, with multiple injuries. The magic circle had gathered to find a way to free her from the self-imposed prison of unconsciousness. Marilee had managed it. She'd shifted into her white wolf and lay down on the altar with Laura at the center of a sacred circle of stones, where all those with magic had gathered to try to help Laura. It had been her daughter's presence that had finally gotten through to Laura. She woke then shifted, for the first time in many years, into her two-legged, human form.

She'd had a lot of wounds from the brutal treatment she'd

received at the hands of her captors, so they had transported her directly to the clinic. The doctor, who was a polar bear shifter, had dressed her wounds and helped her heal. When she was able, he'd also understood her need to go outside and breathe fresh air. The fresh air of freedom.

Laura had made her way slowly to the picnic table, and she had sat there for more than an hour, watching the water and enjoying the air. Gus, one of the magic circle members, had come over to talk to her, and she'd enjoyed their conversation. He was a shaman. Maybe that's why he was so easy to talk to. She wasn't sure how it had happened, but they'd become friends, of a sort, after that first discussion.

Laura saw Marilee crossing the street from the bakery, and she felt her spirit rise with joy. Her daughter had grown into such a lovely young woman. Laura was so proud of the way she'd overcome her rough start in life and had started to take charge of her own future. She worked at the bakery now, helping the three human sisters who owned the place keep it going. All three sisters were newly mated within the past year or two and had less time to spend on the business. Hiring Marilee to help had been a no-brainer.

"I hope you like turkey and roast beef," Marilee said as she sat down opposite Laura and placed two big bags on the picnic table. "I made them myself."

"They smell great," Laura said, accepting the bag that Marilee pushed toward her. "But, sweetheart, I can't keep letting you pay for everything."

"Mine's free. Perk of working there," Marilee explained. "So, I'm only paying for one. And I don't mind at all. You know the prices here are very reasonable. It's not even an hour's worth of tips, honestly."

Laura looked down at the bag. "All the same, I will pay you back as soon as I can figure out how to make some money. I need a job, but I'm twenty years behind on things like computers and technology. I have to find something low-tech."

"I'm sure you could learn computer stuff if you wanted

to," Marilee said kindly. "The folks in this town are really great. They'll teach you, if you need to know something."

"They've been uniformly wonderful, the ones I've met so far," Laura agreed, opening the bag and taking out the sandwich, being sure to anchor the paper with her canned drink so nothing would fly away in the ocean breeze. "I just don't know that there are any job openings."

"Where have you looked so far?" Marilee asked, then took a bite out of her sandwich.

"I went in every shop from the bakery to the end of the main drag heading north. I haven't done the south side, or this side of Main Street yet, but so far, nobody needs any help that I can provide." Laura cringed, then consciously calmed her expression before taking a bite out of her own sandwich.

"Did you work before I was born?" Marilee asked after a short lull while they both chewed and swallowed.

"Not really. We lived very far north in an isolated community. Hard currency wasn't as important there. We traded among ourselves and performed tasks for each other." Laura shrugged. "It was a simpler way of life, modeled on the natives of the area, who lived nearby. We traded with them, too."

"What kinds of things did you trade?" Marilee seemed genuinely interested.

"Things we could get from the land. Wild game, furs, even herbs we could find that they wanted. They traded similar things back, but they were also farmers to some extent, so that's where we got our produce from, a lot of the time. Most of the fresh produce came from greenhouses the local tribe had constructed. Some of our men helped them build, as well. We had a few skilled carpenters. Winter never really left us way up there. A greenhouse was the only way to assure a constant yield to feed their people and have some left over for trade."

"That's really interesting. I didn't expect a native tribe would have been so modern in those days."

Laura laughed. "Honey, it was only twenty years ago. It

wasn't the Stone Age. Greenhouses have been around since Victorian times, after all."

Marilee blushed and ducked her head, eating more of her sandwich. Laura just shook her head. She'd been out of circulation for a while, but she wasn't *that* old. Nothing like kids to make a woman feel her age.

"The biggest problem is that I have no relevant experience working at any of the things the people in this town do," Laura went on, pinpointing her problem. "I want to help out and earn my way, but I'm not sure what I can do. I thought about going up the coast a ways. Maybe there's something I can do where the land is wilder and people aren't so dependent on computers and machines I've never seen before."

"We'll figure something out," Marilee said quickly. "You need to stay here, where it's safe. And I want you here, too. I only just got you back. I don't want you to leave."

"I don't want to leave you either," Laura said, reaching across the table to place her hand over her daughter's. "But, in this modern world, I need money and identity papers. Lots of things I don't have."

"But you do have the most important thing. You have friends here, in Grizzly Cove," Marilee insisted. "And family." Marilee turned her hand over to grasp her mother's. "You've got me and King. Ace, too, and Sabrina. And when their youngest brother gets here, Jack will help, too. You'll see. You've got three strong bear shifter men, who are now part of our family. They'll help. I know they will."

"I love that you've found your true mate, and I'm intrigued at how all these bear shifters get along so well. The few bears I knew before were very solitary," Laura explained. "I just…" She looked away and retrieved her hand, moving it to hold her sandwich once more. "I don't want to be a burden on anyone."

"Never that," Marilee said softly. "You're my mother. My only blood relative. You could never be a burden. You're just a little down right now. I'm sure things will start looking up shortly, and then, you will probably be the one helping me and King. It will all even out in the end. That's the way it's supposed to be with families. I've seen it. Even though I've never experienced it myself."

That broke Laura's heart all over again. "I'm sorry, baby. Of course, I won't leave. But there is a problem, and we have to acknowledge that. I need to be able to pull my weight both in town and within our small family. It'll make me feel better if I can contribute."

"I guess I can understand that," Marilee allowed, "but give yourself a little more time. You're only just healing up from your injuries and tasting freedom for the first time in years. Enjoy that a little before you get too far ahead of yourself, okay?"

Laura shook her head, smiling. How had her little one gotten so wise?

"Okay. You've got a point. I guess I'm just impatient to get on with my life," she admitted.

Marilee laughed. "You don't have to live it all in one day. Take it easy, Mom. You can live on credit for a while yet. And the bears here in Grizzly Cove will probably never try to collect on that debt."

"I will repay it, nonetheless." They ate in silence for a few minutes, enjoying the quiet of the beachfront, the lapping of little waves not too far away. The sandwiches were top notch, too.

Gus saw his quarry sitting at one of the picnic tables down by the water and changed direction. He walked slowly, wanting to give Marilee and Laura as much time together as he could. He knew Marilee would have to be getting back to work soon. It was clear the mother and daughter were enjoying an early lunch before the real rush at the bakery started, and Marilee would have to be inside, serving.

Gus planned to be there when the women finished, so he could tackle his prey—figuratively, of course. Big John had set him a task—to spy on Laura—but it was more than that.

Gus wanted to help her. She had been so vulnerable when she awoke from the self-imposed coma state. She'd been so hurt, both physically and emotionally.

Her physical injuries had healed, mostly, but Gus knew, the mental trauma she had been through wouldn't go away as easily. Since embarking on the shaman's path, Gus had been drawn to help those in need of emotional or spiritual solace. He could no more ignore Laura's situation than he could walk past a trapped bird and not try to help it get free. He *had* to help her. His instincts were screaming at him to offer whatever assistance he could to the beautiful white wolf.

He saw his opportunity as Marilee stood and Laura gathered up the trash from their meal. Marilee took the bag of garbage, then kissed and hugged her mother, and jogged back across the road to the bakery. Laura, as Gus had hoped, stayed for a bit, sipping the drink she hadn't yet finished. Now was his moment.

"Hello," he said, walking up behind her. He knew she had already seen him. She'd turned her head briefly when she first sensed him approach.

"Hi, Gus," she said, still contemplating the water. She'd turned to sit the opposite way on the picnic bench, using the table as a back support as she gazed out at the cove. "Fair warning. You may not want to be around me. I'm in a bit of a grouchy mood."

"Hm. A grouchy werewolf. I guess I can deal with that. We bears can get mighty grouchy ourselves, from time to time." He sat down at the opposite end of the bench she was on, not crowding her, but also not very far apart, either.

Shifters needed closeness. Wolves, even more than bears. He knew that and wanted to provide at least the illusion of solidarity, of caring, that often played a large role in Pack dynamics. Gus had known his share of wolves in his time, and he was more aware of their habits than most bears.

"What rubbed your fur the wrong way today?" he asked, coming right out with his question. He figured she would appreciate the direct approach, and bears were known for their candor.

She turned her head to look at him, leveling him with a sort of bleakness in her steady gaze. "I need to get a job."

He burst out laughing. He couldn't help himself.

"It's not funny," she insisted, turning her nose up as she looked back at the water.

"I'm sorry. I just thought you were going to say something dire and all you need is a job? That's not what I was expecting," he explained, still chuckling.

"It's not as easy as you make it sound. I have no skills. No experience. I've been through half of the stores on Main Street, and nobody needs what little I have to offer." She sounded miserable now, in addition to looking it. That would never do. Gus got serious. Here was a problem that he might be able to help her solve.

"What does Marilee say? You're family. I'm sure she'd be willing to help you—"

She cut him off. "I don't want to be a burden on her. Or anyone, for that matter. I want to pay my own way." He heard the pride in her tone—and the desperation. Maybe this was something she had to do to prove she was no longer a prisoner, even if only in her own mind. "Everyone here has been so kind. Nobody's mentioned how much I owe them, but I'm keeping track, and I'm going to pay them all back. From the girls at the bakery to the man who owns the hotel."

Gus could understand that. Nobody liked to feel like a charity case. He had to figure out some way to get Laura a job. It was clearly important to her, so it was now important to him, as well.

CHAPTER 2

"What are you good at?" Gus asked.

Laura was embarrassed by her background now that she was among these much more sophisticated shifters, but she had to be honest. Bears could sniff out lies, it was said.

"Not much that is valued in this modern world," she admitted, feeling glum. "I was only out of circulation for twenty years, but it might as well have been twenty centuries. I came from a much simpler culture. We didn't use money much. We traded for most things. We lived like our neighbors, the Inuit. Only, we lived closer to the land because we stayed in our beast forms much of the time."

Gus's eyes widened as he looked at her. "Where do you come from, exactly?"

"Up around Ellesmere Island. We are Arctic wolves, after all," she told him, feeling herself smile a little. "There are mountains and glaciers. Lots of snow and ice. That's our natural habitat. White on white, you know?"

"Somehow, I was picturing the more civilized parts of Canada, but clearly, I wasn't thinking," Gus said. "Sorry." He shook his head. "So…Inuit. You have connections to the native people?"

"Very close connections, actually. Those from our Pack who mated humans generally mated with our Inuit neighbors.

My blonde hair and light skin is an anomaly. A gift of my fey ancestry." She tilted her head as she smiled softly. "The majority of my home Pack was darker in human form and, of course, snow white in wolf form. The fey magic makes me even brighter. I never really fit in with the rest of the Pack, but they accepted me and my family. There were a few other blondes, like me, who were my siblings and cousins, parents, grandparents, aunts and uncles. Whoever was touched by the fey magic came out sort of…bleached, I guess you would call it. The elders said the magic of the other realms was too powerful for our mortal forms, and it took its toll over time. My hair was light brown when I was born, and I expect it'll be snow white if I make it to old age. That's not necessarily common for shifters. Usually, we keep our coloration throughout life, even into old age. But the magic acts in strange ways in my line."

"That's interesting," Gus said and she could tell from his tone that he meant it. "So, you're part native, yourself?"

"Definitely," she admitted. "Only those that carried the fey blood were pale, like me. My mother was pale, but her father was a full-blooded Inuit. Son of a tribal elder. My father was a more regular Arctic wolf with Inuit on both sides of his family."

"How did the human mates of the Pack members deal with the climate and harsh conditions that far north?" Gus asked. He sounded genuinely interested, so she opened up a bit more.

"There are mountains up there where people have never been. There are also hidden mountain valleys that have microclimates that make it a little easier to survive the harsh conditions. We would build in those places for our human Pack members and those who wished to live with them. Small settlements, here and there, always tucked away where planes and satellites couldn't see them easily. There's a bit of volcanic activity in some of those areas, and geothermal energy made winters a lot easier," she confided.

"It sounds like a whole other world up there," Gus

marveled, and she could tell by the look of wonder in his eyes that he was impressed. Finally, she didn't feel like such a country bumpkin with no valuable skills. Gus, at least, recognized the ingenuity it took to live wild around the Arctic Circle.

"It can be really beautiful. When the Lights come…" She breathed in a sigh, remembering Mother Nature's light show.

"I've seen the Northern Lights. When I was in Alaska," he told her, and they shared a moment of understanding. "It was one of the moments that led me to my current path."

"That of the shaman?" she asked quietly.

Gus nodded. "I was a soldier for many years. A Special Operator, like most of the men here in town. We all worked together in a special unit made up almost entirely of bear shifters, under the command of an Admiral who knew what we were and what we could do. He also understood why we fought. Not for a country or a political agenda, but for the side of Light. He knew when to send us in…and more importantly, when not to."

She could hardly imagine Gus, sweet, gentle soul that he was, as a soldier. Then, she remembered he was a bear, and she realized he probably had hidden depths, and an enormous strength concealed beneath his calm exterior.

"That's quite a change, from soldier to shaman," she commented.

"It certainly was," he replied. "But it was my calling. I like helping people. I like helping my Clan, and I also help out on the Native American reservation just south of here." He leaned back and looked at her. "Which is where I might be able to help you, too."

She had no idea what he was driving at, but he certainly seemed pleased with himself. Perhaps he had some solution to her problem. Whatever he was thinking, she would listen and make her own judgment.

"How so?" she asked, inviting him to continue.

"Well, I own a building on Main Street that's nearing completion. The inside is ready for tenants, but I've got four spots on the ground floor for small shops and only two interested parties, so far. I wanted to set one of the spaces up for art and jewelry from the res, but we want everyone who works in town to be a resident of Grizzly Cove, and the elders don't really want their people coming up here either. They are respectful of us, but I think there's a bit of fear, too. They pretty much know who and what we are, though we never speak of it." He shook his head, and the ghost of a smile passed his lips. "It's funny, really. Their culture respects shapeshifters, but they're also afraid of us."

"I can understand that," she told him. "The Inuit were like that with my Pack, sometimes, too."

"There are some really amazing artisans whose work is not available anywhere outside their tribe, right now. A couple of them have already approached me about selling some of their jewelry and art in the town during the tourist season, but they want the right person to do the selling. The elders, particularly, want to know the person who will be responsible for the shop. I've already told them I can't do it. I have other responsibilities and can't spend all my time sitting in a store." He shook his head, again. "At the same time, I really want to help them out. The excess items they have—if we were to sell them for them—would bring in some much-needed cash to the artists and the tribe as a whole."

Laura thought about that for a moment. She could see that she wasn't the only one with cash flow problems. She understood—better than the tribal elders would realize—what it meant to be penniless.

"And you think I might be the person to run the store for you?" she asked, uncertain. "Would I have to know computers?"

Gus chuckled. "No computers. At least not right away, and not if you don't want them. But, if you want to learn in the future, I'd be willing to help you." He narrowed his eyes a bit. "Thing is, you'd have to meet at least some of the elders, and maybe a few of the artists. They'd have to approve of you before we could take this any further. Would you be willing to go with me tomorrow? I could set up a quick meeting so they could get to know you a little."

"I can't leave the protection of the ward, right now. I'm still being hunted," she reminded him.

"That's okay. There's a spot at the back of my land where I meet with folks from the res often. They don't mind coming there. My property backs onto the res, and the ward runs around the back of my plot, to the ocean. I live on the piece of land just under the southern point of the cove. I look after the stone circle that's on the point, and my home is just beyond the trees, looking out over the water."

"Sounds nice," she told him. She could just imagine. It sounded divine, but it would be weird if she appeared too enthusiastic.

"I'm just putting the finishing touches on my building in town. You could come take a look at that today, if you want."

She liked the idea of that. Finally, she had hope after a morning of disappointment and worry. She might actually be able to do the job, but she had to learn more first. Seeing the place would go a long way toward easing her anxiety, and she could ask more in-depth questions about her duties.

"Can we go now?" she asked, hoping she didn't sound too needy.

Gus smiled and stood up, holding out a hand to help her in a gentlemanly fashion. "Of course," he replied. "We can walk there if you're up for it. My building is the one right next to the place we just finished a few weeks ago." He pointed to a one of the larger buildings near the apex of the cove on the beach side. "That building has secluded rooms on the lower level where mer can come and go from the water without being seen. They can store their clothing there too. There are rows of lockers, and they've worked out some system among themselves for dolling out the space."

"Intriguing," Laura said as they began walking up to the sidewalk. "I'd wondered how they came and went from the water."

"We put shops on the main floor and hidden passages

down to the lower floor with very private water access," Gus told her. "It seems to work well."

He shrugged as they got to the sidewalk and then turned left, heading past the building he'd just described. Laura took an extra-long look as they passed it, but she couldn't tell from outside that it was any different than it appeared. It certainly didn't look like Mermaid Central, though it apparently was. She shook her head as they passed the front door.

"If you hadn't told me, I never would have guessed," she admitted.

"That's the general idea," Gus replied with a grin. "Now, this… This is my building," he said, stopping at the corner of the building next door and gesturing like a proud papa. "I wanted it to complement the structure next door, though it's a bit smaller and sits just a bit lower on the horizon. We don't want to block too much of the view of the cove, but we also need to camouflage the water entry a bit, with other buildings near it, so it doesn't look too out of place. We want our mer friends to be as safe as possible here."

"I never would have thought about that—putting in other buildings to hide theirs among a group of similar structures," she told him. "This is a lot bigger than I expected. You said there are four smaller shops in the one building?"

"Yes, and apartments on the top floor," he told her. "Notice how you have to go up a small flight of stairs to get to the main floor of the building next door? That's because the upper floor is there to disguise the lower cove access. On my building, the lower floor shops are at ground level, and the upper floor is for living space." They started walking again, and he brought her to the front door. "I've only managed to paint the outside so far. Inside is still a bit rougher and needs some finishing touches, but I'm about ready to let the shop tenants start fixing up their individual spaces."

He opened the door, and they entered the wide, central hall that had four doors leading off of it, right in the center. The back wall had a huge window, overlooking the water with a bench seat beneath. "That's for those who are tired of shopping and just want to sit while the rest of their party goes through the shops."

"What a great idea," she complimented him. "And the view is lovely."

"The two back units will be for mer shops. I have two different tenants already lined up who want to do sea-themed art, jewelry, and gifts. They're eager to get their spaces set up," he told her. "I was going to offer one of the front units to the tribe, but as I said, they want me to man it, and I just don't have the time. I'm talking with another resident about the other unit—a widow and her child. She may need a place for their existing shop while she remodels. She's not happy with the way the workshop area is set up, right now, and may take this smaller space for a few months. She does mostly bamboo art. She's from China, originally. Our one and only adult panda shifter. Her daughter is absolutely adorable in either form."

"I bet." Laura was enchanted by the idea of a tiny panda cub running around the town.

"If Lin doesn't take it, I'm sure I can find someone else to put in the place, at least for the grand opening. After that, we'll see," he went on.

"When is the grand opening?" Laura hadn't realized there was a deadline.

He opened the door of the rooms on the left and let her in. She looked around, taking in the workmanship and how much was left to do.

"I'd like to open as soon as possible, actually. As you can see, it needs paint and a bit of finishing, not to mention the displays need to be set up and arranged. Merchandise has to be brought in and marked with prices. Inventory needs to be taken and some sort of inventory control system set up. I've done some of the preliminary filings with the state and county, so we're getting our paperwork in order, but a lot still needs to be finalized."

"Sounds like a big job." She spun slowly in a circle, taking in the entire space. "It's a very nice design," she said. "I assume that door leads to an office or store room?"

"Go take a look," Gus invited.

Laura went over behind the only counter that had space behind it and opened the door. As she'd suspected, there was both an office area and a small store room.

"I don't anticipate holding a lot of stock in the store room, but I figured there should be some accommodation for duplicate items and supplies," he told her. He'd stayed in the main room while she'd investigated the back room, and she was very aware that he was being the perfect gentleman. The more she was around Gus, the more she liked him.

"It's perfect," she told him, coming back into the main area. "Now, what kind of cash register are you going to have? And what kind of inventory control? Is it some kind of computer stuff that I won't know how to use? Or will good old pen and paper work for you?"

"We can certainly start off with paper books for accounts, but at some point, if you want to move to computer bookkeeping, I'd be happy to help set it up and get you get the proper training. I won't rush you, though. I understand this is all very new to you, and as long as we have a system that works, I don't really care if it's longhand or database." That was music to her ears. "Now, would you be willing to help me paint? I haven't decided on a color scheme, and to be honest, I'm kind of hopeless at decorating. I can design and build the framework, but the finer points of making it look really finished are a bit beyond me."

"I'd be happy to paint. And I can help with some of the trim work, too. I'm not hopeless with a hammer, though I do need a bit of instruction if you want me to do anything fancy," she told him truthfully. "What do you think of a creamy white on the back wall? If you're going to have Native art in here, I'd stick with earth tones and keep it lighter so the room looks bigger. You only have natural light from the big front window in this shop, so you need to keep it bright in here to avoid the walls closing in."

"I like what I'm hearing," Gus told her with an easy grin. "Would you like to see the apartments up top? They're pretty much ready, except for the paint. But everything else is in and working."

"Sure, why not?" Laura went with him out the door of the shop and back toward a door that was mostly hidden in the hallway.

It opened onto a staircase that wound upward. When they reached the top, she was in a smaller hallway with four doors roughly matching the shops below. He opened the one on the back of the building, and they went in.

Laura stopped short in the doorway. The living room, which was the first room they entered, was dominated by large windows that looked out over the cove. The view was stunning from up here. There was furniture already in place. A sectional couch in neutral gray tones sat in front of the windows, with smaller chairs arranged beside it in a conversational grouping.

Across from that was an open kitchen area, with white cabinets, gray tile, and stainless steel appliances. Just big enough for the size of the apartment. Not too small, not too large. A breakfast bar with stone countertops and high stools made the area cozy.

"The bedrooms are back here," Gus said, leading the way back past the kitchen area. "Two bedrooms and one bathroom in each unit," he said, giving her the grand tour. "I figured one bedroom could be used as a guest room or office, if the renter is single. We have a lot of single bears in town, still, even though quite a few of our brothers have found their mates. Mated pairs usually want their own lair on their own territory, so the apartments are meant for bachelors, mostly. And mer. Some of them like to have places on land, as well as in the sea."

CHAPTER 3

Laura peeked into the doorways of each of the three rooms in the back. The bathroom was done in that same light gray and white theme, and only one of the larger rooms had been done up as a bedroom. The other was empty. The bedroom needed finishing. There was a large bed there, but little else. No curtains, for example, though Laura noticed packages on the bed that looked like grey and white curtains and silver rods. They just had to be put up.

"This place is lovely. I know you said you weren't good at decorating, but I love this gray and white motif. It's very calming," she told him.

He shook his head. "Urse picked out the finishes. I needed all the help I could get picking colors and styles of tile and fabric. She picked out the furniture, as well."

"Well, she has great taste," Laura replied as they walked back into the main area. "This place is gorgeous."

"Look, I know you're staying at the hotel," Gus said, looking a bit pained as he brought up a subject that was a bit irritating to her at the moment.

She didn't like being a freeloader at the hotel, but there was simply no place else for her, right now. Her daughter was newly mated, but they'd only just purchased their own property, and the house wasn't even built yet. They were both still living in the hotel, too.

"I am," Laura said, bristling a bit.

"This place is empty, and if you wanted to move in here, I'd be grateful. I need someone to oversee the building. You're a level-headed woman. I think I can trust you to be sort of the den mother for those who will be renting from me, both up here in the apartments and down in the shops. I would give you the apartment rent-free as long as you were willing to run interference for me with the tenants."

"Seriously?" That slipped out before she could censor her response.

It seemed really too good to be true, but by the same token, he was a busy man with responsibilities to both the town and the nearby Native tribe. He probably did need help, and she certainly needed to be earning her own way. Maybe this was meant to be.

"I mean…" She tried again. "If it's really worth that much to you, I suppose I could at least give it a try. You know, my daughter and King might want to rent one of the apartments from you while they're building their house. Would it be all right if I mentioned that possibility to them?"

"Certainly," Gus replied. "I know what the motel charges, and I'm friendly with the owner. As tourist season draws closer, he's probably going to need as many rooms as he can clear for transient guests, so it might be a good solution all the way around."

He went on to name a sum for monthly rent that wasn't too high, and not too low to be insulting. It was a fair price, and she thought it was also fair to count that as her compensation for taking care of his property. They were basically doing a trade, which was something she was very comfortable with. She would keep his property running smoothly and help all the tenants in return for a roof over her head. This could really work.

Gus was pleased with the way things had turned out. Laura had agreed to move to the apartment and take care of the building. She would also run the shop, contingent on her approval by the tribal elders. Gus left her, feeling as if he'd accomplished a great deal, and went on to schedule a meeting for the next day between the elders and Laura. As long as they gave her the nod of approval, his plan to get her where he could keep an eye on her more easily might actually work.

He felt a little strange about essentially conning the woman into moving into his building and running his business, but he knew it was ultimately for the good of the Clan. Big John didn't often ask for favors, and Gus liked to accommodate him whenever possible. John was a good Alpha, a good leader. He had identified Laura as a possible threat to the stability of the community. Gus might disagree, but he had to admit, John had a right to be worried. It was, after all, his job and his vocation to worry about every soul that came under his protection.

That's why, against his better judgment, Gus had agreed to keep an eye on Laura. Better him than anybody else. At least Gus would try to be kind if it turned out that she was some sort of sleeper agent. He knew her, and her circumstances, well enough by now to truly believe that she was a good person at heart. She would not knowingly try to hurt anyone in this town.

She might have good reason to want to rip the heads off of those who had kept her prisoner for so very long, but those evil beings were out of her reach for now. At this moment in time, her first task was to heal and mend the unavoidable rift from her only child. This was time for quiet reflection, soul searching, and getting to know her grown daughter. Reestablishing family ties that should never have been broken in the first place.

Gus arranged the meeting with the tribal leadership, and they all agreed to come around to his place the next day. Gus called Laura at the hotel to give her the good news and tell her what time to expect him. He'd offered to pick her up at the hotel and bring her out to his place, since she didn't have her own independent transportation. Sooner or later, she'd have to get something. Even a bicycle would make getting from one end of the town to the other much easier on her healing body. He'd have to look into what might be available. Maybe he'd talk with Ace and King. Perhaps they had something in mind for Laura, and if not, as the town's new mechanics, they would be the most likely to be able to get something for her quickly.

Perhaps they hadn't thought about it. If not, Gus was going to put the bug in their ears and get them to start considering what the new womenfolk in their lives might need in the way of transport. Their spouses, of course, and the extended family—namely, Laura—as well.

Gus would be happy to pay for a car for Laura, but he wasn't sure how that would be received. She'd accepted the possibility of the apartment, only because he had convinced her that her presence in the building, as den mother, was a fair trade. He would pay her for her work in the shop, though they hadn't discussed a salary yet. But he wasn't sure how he could justify giving her a car in such a way as to not make her feel beholden to him.

It was important to let her keep her pride. She was literally a stranger in a strange land. She came from a more primitive culture and had been imprisoned for over twenty years. Whatever skills she might have had were dated and probably not readily applicable to modern life. He'd have to tread carefully, so as not to insult her.

The next morning, Laura was ready and waiting for him in the hotel lobby, just before lunchtime. He'd invited the elders for a backyard luncheon where they could get to know Laura in a relaxed setting. He was sure they would be asking her tough questions about her past and her ties with the Inuit. It was important to some of the old-timers that they have someone with Native blood bringing their art to the world.

Gus, himself, had only a little Native American ancestry, but they'd accepted him mostly, he thought, because of his chosen path as a shaman. They probably knew he was also a shapeshifter, though nobody spoke of it aloud. The elders respected his privacy—and that of the entire community of Grizzly Cove, for that matter.

He suspected they actually liked having magical folk—especially shifters with bear spirits—nearby. It helped them keep their belief in the old ways and teach the younger generation. Occasionally, Gus would let himself be seen by some of the younger Native kids. His light fur always got a reaction, and he knew the kids carried the story of seeing the Spirit Bear back to their families, friends, and neighbors.

Gus didn't mind. It was part of being what he was. A rare kind of bear—a Spirit Bear. His fur was much lighter than a grizzly's, and his kind were considered sacred by some. At the very least, seeing him was a special treat for the res kids who didn't have a lot of real magic in their lives. He liked seeing them smile and giving them hope that maybe magic was real, after all.

"This is a nice truck," Laura said as she easily made the climb into the cab of Gus's white pickup.

She was lithe and muscular like most shifters. Getting up into the cab wasn't hard for her, he was glad to see. His pickup was one of his few indulgences. It was big and roomy, and he kept it sparkling whenever possible.

"Thanks," he said easily. "I think most of the elders are coming for lunch. You should feel honored. I didn't tell them about your background. I figured you'd like to do that yourself. Thing is, they're going to want to know about your aboriginal ties. They want an authentic Native selling their wares. I'm not sure exactly why, but it's important to them, and I respect their wishes in such matters."

"No problem. I'm just glad they're giving me a chance. I need a break, you know?"

She sounded anxious, which he didn't like. His inner bear wanted to growl. Gus settled for reaching across the distance that separated them and taking her hand in his.

"It'll be okay. We'll figure this out. I promise." He was promising a lot more than she realized, but that was for him to know, at this point.

Laura was a shattered soul, and he wanted desperately to help her put herself back together and fully heal. The more he was around her, the more that became a mission central to his own happiness. He didn't know why. It just was.

She smiled at him, but he could tell she was still nervous. Thankfully, they arrived at his place, and he parked the truck. She'd already climbed down before he got out, but she was an independent woman, and he had to respect that, much as he'd like to coddle her in every possible way.

"So…" she said, looking around. "You're making lunch? Is there anything I can do to help?"

"Sure. We have some time before they get here. You can help me make a salad, if you like." Gus led the way into his house.

He'd never had a woman here. Not since he'd finished building the place. He felt a little odd about inviting Laura into his lair, but soon got over it. She was good company. Quiet and respectful of his territory, but also fun to be around when she chose to talk and share bits about her prior life.

They worked together to prepare the food, but when he fired up the grill outside on the deck, she took over. He had prepared fish and steak. She went right for the fish, setting them up on the open flame like a pro.

"I hope you don't mind," she told him. "Where I come from, women are the better cooks, most of the time, and we eat a lot of fish."

"What other things did you eat up there? Walrus?" Gus ventured.

"Occasionally," she agreed while she worked. "Lots of caribou. Once in a while, we'd trade for whale, from the neighboring tribe. But, most of the time, we lived off whatever we could find."

"That must have been quite the life," he told her, amazed all over again, that this woman had lived up near the top of the world where few humans, and even fewer shifters, dared to tread.

The table was laid, and the other dishes had been put out by the time the elders started arriving. They came overland, on quad bikes, and the oldest of the group traveled together in an ancient Jeep. They parked their vehicles at the edge of Gus's property then walked in on foot. Gus went to greet them and help the one really old guy navigate the grass.

He'd come to know these people over the past couple of years, and this wasn't the first time he'd had them all over to share a meal. One of the elderly ladies, a sweetheart named Betty Two Feathers, carried a box that smelled sweet to Gus. She must have brought dessert. Sky Bunty, one of the older men, had a hamper with something else that smelled delicious inside. They hadn't come empty-handed to his home, which was very thoughtful of them.

He introduced them all to Laura, but she was still kind of busy with the fish, which turned out to be a good thing as Betty and her cohort, Fern Rasmussen, joined Laura by the grill. They started discussing preparation techniques, and Laura told them how they did things up north. She explained how they fished through holes in the ice and how they used every part of the caribou. Gus could see she had easily charmed the ladies, but it might still take some convincing for the men, who were in the majority of this particular group.

When lunch was ready, they all sat down together to eat. Gus said a few words in his role as shaman and host, and soon, the food was disappearing and conversation abounded. Laura was quiet except for when Fern or Betty asked her questions or made comments. They sat on either side of her, like guardians. Gus suppressed his grin. Those two old biddies hadn't taken to him so easily.

"I understand you have Inuit blood," Ray Parker, the oldest of the men here, came out and addressed the topic directly, speaking to Laura for the first time. He was a bit of a loudmouth, Gus had always thought, but Ray spoke his mind plainly, and Gus respected that.

Laura nodded. "On both sides, though I take after my

mother, who was fair, like me."

"But how? Did a bunch of crazy white explorers marry into the tribe?" he asked, almost challengingly.

Laura looked surprised. "No," she said quietly. "It's probably the fey blood."

Everybody fell silent, staring from her to Gus and back again. Gus tried to intervene, but it was clear there was no going back from what had just been revealed.

"Uh…I don't know how it is up north," Gus said into the silence, "but down here, we don't really talk about such things, Laura. Not out in the open, and not with…uh…non-magical folk," he tried to explain gently.

"Oh, my." Laura paled. "I'm so sorry. I thought they knew about us, and about the town."

Gus shook his head. She was digging them in deeper, not helping matters.

"What about the town, dear?" Betty asked before Gus could figure a way to stop this rolling snowball.

"About all the shifters," Laura said, blinking innocently. "I think I'm one of only two werewolves in town, but I can't be sure. Everyone else seems to be some kind of bear."

Gus dropped his chin to his chest in despair.

It was Betty who broke the silence. She laughed. Chuckling, at first, then laughing outright in loud guffaws as the rest of them joined in. Tears were running down her face as she looked at Gus.

"Oh, sonny, we knew about you all along. You're not the only one who can sense things around here. We just never really talked about it. We figured, if you didn't mention it, we wouldn't bring it up." She sobered slowly, as did the rest of the group. "You're the Spirit Bear, aren't you? The one my grandson keeps seeing crossing the old stream by the giant sequoia grove."

Gus was more than a bit uncomfortable. This was something he'd never thought would be spoken of aloud. He'd thought they would fear him, if his true nature was ever confirmed. Instead, they just seemed curious. Big John was going to have a canary when Gus filed his report about this later, but for now, he decided to go with it and see where it led.

"My Alpha's going to kill me, but yes, I'm a Spirit Bear," Gus confirmed. It felt like a weight had been lifted from his shoulders the minute the words were out. Huh. He hadn't expected that. Maybe this was the right thing to do, after all.

"Grizzly sightings have been way up since you boys came to the area, too," one of the men put in. "We don't normally have that many big bears in the region, so we sort of put two and two together a while back. I hope you don't mind."

"Mind?" Gus's voice rose to a very high pitch. He couldn't believe this. Not in his wildest dreams had he ever imagined a conversation quite like this.

"I guess there are rules about revealing ourselves to non-magic folk, but I've never been this far south before, so I'm not sure," Laura put in, trying to be helpful. "Up where I'm from, there just aren't that many people, and most of the Inuit know all about us. It's kind of hard to hide when many of my Pack find mates among the local people."

"You carry the spirit of the white wolf," Fern said, as if it was something she said every day. "And something else. This fey, you mentioned? Is that like fairies? Little winged things that flit about doing magic?"

Laura tilted her head, as if considering. Gus couldn't wait to hear how she was going to handle this one. The conversation had taken a surreal turn, and he didn't know how to get it back to normality.

"I've never seen a full-blooded fey, myself. Just my extended family, who carry the blood in various stages of dilution. I've been taught that the fey are not of this realm, but they can sometimes travel between realms to affect things here. One of my ancestors was fey, and his magic shows through in each generation. It is said he was tall and blond, paler than the most fair-skinned human, with blue eyes and pointed ears. He was a warrior who fell in love with my ancestor and stayed here in the mortal realm with her, while she lived. He was highly magical, and therefore, so is my line. The magic bleaches our color out a little more, the older we get. I was born with brown hair and much darker skin. My eyes were always light because I'm a white wolf, and many of us always had light eyes."

"So, you are more Native than you look," Ray stated rather rudely. Then, the man laughed. "Heck, you're probably more Native than I am." He continued to laugh as he sat back in his chair. "She's okay with me, if you want to give her the job."

That seemed to galvanize them all into a vote. In short order, Laura was confirmed as the tribe's agent to sell their artwork and jewelry in Gus's gallery in Grizzly Cove. He couldn't believe it had all happened so fast. He also still couldn't believe how easily they had accepted what should have been forbidden knowledge.

CHAPTER 4

Without even asking, Justin Tall Pines, who was the youngest member of the tribal council and represented the artisans of the group, went back to the Jeep. He came back with two boxes filled with items the artists had entrusted with him to sell outside the tribe. Precious silver and turquoise jewelry. Small art pieces. Handsome dream catchers with feathers and beads. Lots of pretty things that would sell well to the tourist trade.

Betty and Fern took charge of showing the items and explaining their origin to Laura. She appeared to be listening carefully and handled each item with great reverence, as the rest of the group watched closely. Gus could see minute nods of approval as she asked pertinent questions that helped her understand the items better.

When they came to a small selection of carved horn, she didn't need any coaxing. Laura explained that she was very familiar with the art of scrimshaw. In fact, it was something she had done many years ago, as a young girl and on into adulthood. She sounded truly excited for the first time since Gus had met her. Perhaps he could get her started on carving again. Maybe it would be therapeutic, and also, maybe it could be a way for her to make a little extra money, since that seemed to be a major problem for her, just now.

The elders seemed to agree. Justin went back to the vehicles and returned with a small box of antler pieces. He gave the box to Laura with great ceremony.

"I collect antlers when they drop," he told her. "Maybe this is enough to get you started carving again."

Laura looked touched, and Gus could see there were tears in her eyes as she accepted the gift. She thanked Justin and promised she would not forget the kindness he had just shown her. Gus knew she would look for a way to repay the man—whether in cash or in barter goods. It was just her way.

"I have some carving tools you can borrow," Gus told her, and everyone seemed to approve of the idea. They opened the box with the dessert in it—a confection of honey, nuts and dried fruits—and they shared it around while everyone talked.

Gus had never felt more welcome among these people. There was still a bit of reserve between them, but they were more open and relaxed now, than they had ever been with him. Perhaps that was Laura's doing. Either her presence here had made them loosen up, or, more likely, her candor had brought the secrets out in the open and made everyone more comfortable with where they stood. As they ate dessert, Gus felt the need to clarify a few things with everybody.

"Just so we're clear, there is a very strict prohibition against shifters discussing our true nature with humans," Gus told them during a lull in the conversation. "Please don't go telling everybody about us. That could bring a lot of trouble to more than just this town, but to many innocent people, all over the world."

"Oh, don't worry about us," Betty told him. "Who'd believe us anyway? Most of the outside world looks at us and thinks were just a bunch of crazy Indians who believe in hocus pocus." They all got a good laugh at that.

"All right," Gus allowed, smiling to soften his words. "But it's really important. Laura has been…well…out of circulation for a long time and isn't from anywhere even remotely around here, in the first place. She wasn't aware of our traditions and restrictions. I can't blame her for speaking the truth, but it really isn't done."

"We understand," Ray piped up. "But it's better to have the truth between us, at last. We liked you from the start, even before we guessed you had the bear spirit within you. You have always honored our ways, and you have been making a good effort to help our people. We respect that. And we appreciate the respect you have shown us in return."

Gus was floored by what had happened, but as the luncheon drew to an end, he thought it had turned out about as well as he could have hoped. The elders had not only approved of Laura...they *adored* her. They had also been more accepting about the revelations regarding himself, and magic in general, than he ever could have dreamed.

He still wasn't sure how he was going to explain this all to Big John, but he'd find a way. He'd especially try to find a way that didn't implicate Laura. She hadn't realized what she'd said could be dangerous. Maybe it was a cultural difference. Or maybe it was just those many years she had spent essentially comatose and under enemy control. Whatever the reason, Gus wanted to cut her some slack. He wasn't sure the rest of the Clan would be as understanding.

The words had been said. The tribe was aware. The die had been cast. What happened now, was anyone's guess.

Laura felt like she drifted through the rest of that day. After lunch, Gus had taken her back to the hotel, only to give her a chance to pack her things and then take her straight over to the apartment. She felt like she was living a dream when he left her at the apartment with a promise to return to pick her up for a celebratory dinner later. He gave her all the keys to the building and free reign with the premises. He'd shown her where the master switches were for things like the electricity and the water main, then left her to get settled.

She didn't have many possessions. Just the few things she'd gathered since waking. Some clothes that had been donated to her by the townsfolk. Some that had been gifted to her by her daughter. A few basic toiletries. Not much to show for a life, but she was slowly getting a foothold on being human, again.

She had stayed in wolf form a very long time. A wolf's needs were much simpler, but it was nice to be walking on two legs again, even if there were a lot more rules and requirements of this form. She felt bad about blurting out the news about shifters and her fey ancestry in front of the elders. She hadn't been around non-magical humans in so long, she hadn't really thought about it, but she knew she'd broken shifter law. She was just lucky the people she'd informed had already suspected and could be trusted not to go blabbing to the rest of the mortal world about the existence of shifters living among them.

She felt a lot better about her prospects after meeting with them. She had liked the elders. They all had a good feeling about their spirits. Good auras. She would enjoy working for the betterment of their people, and she had come to tears when that one man—Justin—had given her the box of antler pieces for carving. What a sweet, sweet man.

Gus had thrown a few carving tools into the box with the antlers before they'd left his home, and she couldn't wait to see what she had. She had missed the quiet times when she could just create something pretty and let her imagination run wild. She had learned to carve on bone as a young girl and had become good enough that the hunters would give her walrus tusk to work with on occasion. She had loved carving ivory, but Justin had mentioned how it was illegal now, except in rare instances.

That was a good thing, to her mind. Too many animals had been slaughtered by mortals, just for their ivory. At least when her people took an animal—a walrus or a caribou or whatever else they could find—it was done with respect, and because they needed it to survive. They didn't let any part go to waste. It wasn't done for sport or for ivory. That kind of killing wasn't right, in her mind. Her wolf spirit was a true carnivore, but that killer instinct was tempered by her human side, which abhorred killing just for the sake of killing.

Laura had put her few things away and had a good look around the apartment before settling by the window overlooking the cove with her precious box of antler pieces and tools. She opened it like she was opening a precious gift and was pleased to find tools she recognized in there. She could definitely work with this.

The first thing she wanted to do was make something for Justin, who had shown her such kindness in giving her the raw material to work with. She would carve him a scene from her homeland. Wolves running across the snow, hunting a mighty caribou. She could already see it in her mind as she set to work.

It was hours later when Gus knocked on the apartment door. Laura had lost track of time while working on her first carving in more than two decades. It wasn't nearly ready yet, but she was already proud of her work. She hadn't lost the knack, it seemed. She quickly cleaned up and went to answer the door.

She didn't have many changes of clothes, so she couldn't dress up for dinner, but Gus didn't seem to mind. He took her to the only restaurant in town, which was called Flambeau's. Zak Flambeau, the owner and head chef, waved at them as they came in, then went back into the kitchen where two others were also cooking. The scents wafting from that door made her mouth water, but the hint of spice in the air almost made her eyes water. There weren't a lot of spices way up north, so she wasn't used to hot peppers and the other exotic flavors Zak apparently liked to use.

"Is everything spicy here?" Laura asked Gus in an undertone she hoped didn't carry too far. She didn't want to insult anyone.

"Zak is Cajun, so that's his specialty, but they'll cook things just about any way you want, if you ask. Not everyone likes chili peppers," Gus said, smiling kindly.

When she looked at the menu, the prices seemed high, but she really didn't have any frame of reference. She had never lived in a city for very long and hadn't been free for decades. There was so much she had to learn. And she suspected any prices would seem high to someone who had no money.

"This dinner is my treat," Gus said out of the blue. She looked up at him quickly. Had he somehow read her mind? He'd probably interpreted the look on her face as she perused the menu.

"I can't let you," she said. "You've already done so much."

"No arguments," he replied, smiling at her, though his words were firm. "Tonight is a celebration. My building can finally be put to use. I built the thing on spec, and frankly, it's cost me a lot of money to this point, without actually making any return on the investment. If you can get it ready for business by the time tourists start to roll through, I might actually start to earn something for my efforts. So will you, and so will the tribe. It'll be good, all the way around." His enthusiasm was almost infectious. "Let's just enjoy a meal and celebrate our good fortune in getting this project moving, finally, and all the good things I hope will come of it."

"Well, when you put it that way, I'd be churlish to refuse," she told him. "But, once I earn a little money, I'll want to return the favor."

"You're on," he agreed easily. Too easily? She wasn't sure. Was he just fobbing her off, or was he as eager to spend more time in her company as she was to be with him? And wouldn't that beat all?

She had honestly thought her chance at flirtation and attraction was over. She was a widow. She'd lost her mate. She'd believed he'd been her true mate. Marilee was evidence of that. But, if that was the case, why was Laura feeling an undeniable attraction tugging her toward Gus?

Shifters only got one mate—if they were very, very lucky. If her handsome young mage had been her true mate, she should not be attracted to any other man. Ever.

And yet, there was no denying the fact that long-dormant feelings were rising. She wouldn't act on them, but she was definitely feeling an attraction, the more she was around Gus.

It was a puzzle, to be sure.

She was precluded from thinking about it as the waiter came over and took their orders. Laura opted for something without a lot of spice. Just a plain cut of meat, lightly seared with butter, a side of steamed vegetables and a baked potato. That was plenty of flavor for her reawakening taste buds.

Before the waiter had even left the table, King and Marilee walked in the door of the restaurant. When they spotted Laura and Gus, they came right over. Gus invited them to join them, and things were quickly rearranged to include the younger couple, much to Laura's delight. She loved being around her daughter. Marilee was so obviously happy with King, the two of them just shone with the light of love. It was incredibly refreshing after so long in the darkness.

"Is it okay to tell them about today?" Laura asked Gus, not wanting to put her foot in her mouth again. She would check with him first, from now on, before revealing anything to anyone, if at all possible.

Gus smiled, giving her a bemused look. "Sure. They'll all know sooner or later, and I've already got the approval of the town council."

Marilee was watching her mother with an inquisitive smile. King was harder to read, but friendly as she told them about having lunch with the tribal elders in Gus's backyard. Laura didn't miss the speculative look Marilee shot Gus at that particular revelation, but Laura went on with her news quickly, hoping to sidetrack any questions in that direction.

"I think Gus just about fainted when I told them I had fey blood," Laura said, and she saw Marilee's eyes widen. Even her daughter's stoic mate started a bit, his shoulders tensing. "I didn't know it was forbidden to speak of such things. Where I come from, the Native people knew all about us. We lived side by side, in harmony with each other and with nature. We also intermarried a lot, so there really was no way to keep it secret when the Pack spent so much time in our fur due to the weather conditions. Only those with human mates stayed two-legged for long stretches, to be with their

41

beloved."

Marilee gazed at her with wide eyes. "It sounds like something out of another century."

"It is, at times. Survival hasn't changed all that much, though modern materials always found a way up there to the people who needed them. It just took a while, and supplies were scarce. The things they'd always used—things from the land and sea—were more readily available, so they're probably still in use today in many places," Laura reasoned. "If things ever calm down enough, I'd love to go up to Ellesmere and see if I can find anybody I know. I had a pretty large extended family. Cousins and aunts and uncles. My grandparents were still alive when I left. I wonder if they're still around?"

Laura's voice trailed off as she thought about that. It was Gus who restarted the conversation a moment later. "I had to report what had happened at lunch to Big John, of course. Up to today, I had no idea that the tribe knew anything concrete, but you should have heard the hooting and hollering when I explained to Laura that our existence is supposed to be secret."

"Apparently, it's one of the worst kept secrets around," Laura put in. "They mentioned that they noticed the sudden rise in bear sightings. Since it happened right around the time the town was settled, they said they'd put two and two together a long time ago. And this one," Laura pointed to Gus, smiling as she did so, "has been sighted, again and again, near a grove of giant sequoias. Not very subtle, Gus, when you have white fur. Ask me. I know."

They all chuckled at her words, and Gus had the grace to look a little sheepish. The waiter arrived with their appetizers, and the conversation was put on hold for a moment. When the table had settled again, and they all had small plates of chosen tidbits in front of them, Gus picked up the thread of what he'd been saying.

"Big John wasn't happy about any of it," Gus told them. "But he did say that, if anyone had to find out, he was glad they were Native Americans. Shifter communities used to work closely with the indigenous peoples in the old days, according to John's research. It was pretty clear, from their reaction, the old timers still had enough belief in their ancestors' stories that they didn't get upset when they started suspecting the presence of bear shifters in the neighborhood a few years ago. If they hadn't, things would have gone quite differently when the town was first settled. As it is, John is going to have to tell the rest of the town council about this, but he doesn't think there will be any problems. We just need to be more careful from here on out."

Laura breathed a sigh of relief. "Thank heaven for that," she muttered, but they all heard her, of course. Shifter hearing wasn't easily foiled. She decided a change of subject was in order. "I've moved out of the hotel," she announced, and Marilee looked shocked.

"What? Why? Did someone say something?" Bless her, Marilee looked like she was ready to do battle on Laura's behalf. Just when she thought she had her shy daughter figured out, she reacted in a way Laura didn't expect, but found utterly adorable.

"It's fine," Laura insisted. "I took a job running one of the boutiques in Gus's new building on Main Street, and he's letting me stay in one of the apartments for free, as long as I act as den mother for the building. I think I'm getting the better end of that trade, for sure." She smiled at Gus then looked back at her daughter. "The place is gorgeous, and there are three more just like it, still empty and looking for renters. I thought maybe you two might want to look at one of the units as a place to stay while your house is coming together. The hotel, while comfortable, has got to be a little confining for newlyweds, no? And we could be neighbors. At least until your house is done."

"I like that idea," Marilee said immediately. "Maybe we could come take a look tomorrow?" She looked to her mate, and King nodded.

"Is there a particular time that would be convenient,

ma'am?" King asked Laura.

"Oh, anytime is good. I'll be there all day, working on getting the shop ready. Just come into the front left side shop and holler if you don't see me right away. I might be in the back room," she replied.

Gus told them the rent number he was thinking about, and Laura was glad to see that neither her daughter nor King flinched at the amount. This might just work out, after all.

They shared a companionable dinner together, and Gus insisted on picking up the tab for all of them when they were through. He really was a generous and kind soul. Laura vowed in her own mind to do the best possible job she could for him. He was so good to give her this chance, she wouldn't squander it.

They parted with the younger couple on the street in front of the restaurant. They had Marilee's SUV in the parking lot, and they would drive back to the hotel on the other end of town. As for Gus and Laura, the new building was just across the street and down a ways. The night was cool, but not too cold for a pair of shifters. Gus walked her back to the building and escorted her right up to the apartment door.

She opened her door, and he peered in, sniffing audibly. She was sure he could scent if anyone had been in there since she'd left. So could she, for that matter, but it was polite of him to look out for her safety, even if it probably wasn't necessary in a town with a permanent ward against evil.

Regardless, she could smell the apartment was as she'd left it. She was safe. She turned to him, and the smile slid from her face at the serious expression in his eyes. Was he…?

Hot damn. He was angling in for a kiss.

Laura decided to just let it happen and see what it felt like. She hadn't kissed a man since her mate, and she'd thought she would never want another's kiss ever again, but… Gus was a very tempting man.

His lips met hers, and she swooned. There was no other word for it. Her knees buckled, and she felt lightheaded, but she managed to stay on her feet—probably mostly due to the fact that his arms had wrapped around her waist and he was holding her up. She found his strength sexy, and his kiss… It was unbelievable. Magical. Mystical. Deliciously tempting. Much like the man, himself.

And then, it was over. Gus held her until her knees steadied then let go of her by slow degrees, holding her gaze all the while.

"Good night, Laura," he said, his voice a growly, husky whisper of masculine sound that reverberated through her weakened knees and made her innards clench with sudden desire. "Sleep well, sweetheart."

She couldn't find her voice to reply, so stunned was she by the unexpected sensual haze. Damn. The man could pack a punch.

CHAPTER 5

The next morning when Laura left the apartment and went downstairs to investigate the shop, it was clear that Gus, or someone, had been there already. Probably while she'd been in the shower. The evidence was clear. There were several cans of paint in various shades of cream and taupe and a pile of painting equipment on top of the counter by the door to the back room.

Laura looked over the paint and tools with enthusiasm. While her people didn't generally paint their homes the way the people here did, they were all about decorative painting of objects. Usually small objects. Her earliest painting had been done with hues they could make from things around them. Certain plants and even clay. This would be her first time attempting something large, like an entire shop, and she knew Gus probably expected her to pick just one of the colors he'd supplied and do the whole place with it, but she thought maybe she could come up with something a little better.

An idea in mind, she set to work. She thought she could get a good portion of one wall done today so she had something to show Gus. If he didn't like it—or if it didn't come out as she envisioned—it would be easy enough to just paint over it all with the big roller. In the meantime, she was going to enjoy getting her hands dirty. She set to work and didn't surface again, until late afternoon when King and Marilee dropped by to take a look at the apartment.

She had a good time showing them around the building, but they didn't step into the gallery. She wanted Gus to be the first to see what she was doing there. If he didn't like it, she would just paint over it, and it would be as if it had never been there. She would give him the option. It was his building, after all.

Marilee and King liked what they saw from all accounts and left with smiles and promises to think about moving. Laura prayed her daughter and new son-in-law would join her in the otherwise empty building. She liked having family around, and her inner wolf needed Pack…perhaps more than she would admit. She went back to work in the gallery with a hopeful feeling, immersing herself in her art.

Laura was so intent on her work that she didn't look up when she heard the outer doors open and close. She could hear Gus's voice and smell his delicious scent, so she knew it was okay. He had others with him. Two people that smelled of kelp and ocean water. They must be mer, she thought idly, while she put the finishing touches on her composition.

She heard their footsteps—not Gus's, but the mermaids' light footfalls—going toward the back of the building. They must be the tenants Gus had lined up for the two seaward-facing galleries. She kept working while their voices and sounds dissipated toward the back of the big building and put them out of her mind.

The next thing she knew, the outer door of her shop opened, and Gus's scent wafted in. He was here!

Gus took one look at the wall Laura was painting and stifled a gasp. He hadn't expected this. Instead of picking one of the neutral hues he'd left and going at the blank wall with a roller, she'd painted a…a masterpiece…on the small section of wall next to the door that led to the back room. Not the side that had the display cabinet and would house the register, but the blank wall on the other side.

She'd done a winter scene in taupe and cream. Subtle shade on shade coloring depicting what must be a memory of her homeland. The mural depicted a snowy, windswept mountain range in the distance and a white wolf just visible closer in. He felt chilly just looking at it, the image evoking a very strong feeling in him. This was *art*. Laura was a true artist.

"Do you like it?" He heard her voice as if from afar. He'd been transported for a moment out of time into the wild, snowy world of her youth.

"Like it?" He cleared his throat, swallowing past the dryness. "Laura, this is…it's…unbelievable."

She cringed. "You don't like it. I'm sorry." She turned and picked up the big paint roller. "I can just paint over it."

"No!" He hadn't meant to shout. Gus moderated his tone at her confused expression. "No, please don't. It's stunning. Beautiful. Almost magical." He stepped closer. "How did you do this?"

"Well, there were two smaller brushes, and I did the background color with the roller, but for the rest…" She held up her hands and the tip of every finger had a different shade on it.

"You finger-painted *that*?" He was stunned. If she could do that kind of art with her fingers, what could she do with proper brushes? It boggled the mind.

She shrugged. "It's more abstract this way, but I enjoy feeling the paint on my hands. I was careful not to drip."

"Drips are the least of my concerns. Honey, this is… I'm at a loss for words because it's so beautiful." He turned to her and smiled at the way her expression filled with delight.

"Really?" She set down the roller in the tray of paint, and he could see a becoming little blush on her cheeks. "You really like it?"

"I *love* it," he told her honestly. "It's just what this place needs. You're a genius." He came over and put his arms around her, giving her a warm hug. "Thank you for using your talent to beautify this space." He placed a kiss on the top of her head. She was shorter than him, but she fit his arms perfectly. "You know, with talent like this, you could sell your own art here in the gallery."

She leaned back to look up at him. "You think so?"

"Definitely. If you want it, this wall can be all yours, to display your art." He gestured toward the beautifully painted wall, taking in the wonder of her work once more. "And I think I finally have a name for this gallery. What would you say if we called it the White Wolf Gallery, in your honor?"

"Seriously?" Her breath caught before she went on. "I really would be honored. But what about...you know...keeping the shifter secret? Isn't it a little too obvious?"

Gus shrugged as she moved out of his embrace. "I'm already calling this building Spirit Bear House. The majority of the world will just think it's a Native American name. Only other shifters will understand the real significance. Any tourists we get coming through will probably just think it's quaint. And the mural explains the name of this particular gallery. Maybe you can design a logo for the shop with just the wolf? I'll pay you a fair price for your art," he promised.

She looked taken aback, as if she hadn't expected to be paid for her art. He found that both troubling and adorable. She would have to learn the ways of this modern world if she was going to survive here. He would do all he could to gently coach her in what she needed to know.

"Well, I'm flattered, but I told you I'd paint your place. It's part of the deal," Laura insisted.

"When we talked about painting the gallery, I never expected you were an artist. I thought you would just pick a color and do the whole place that one color. This... This is above and beyond what I thought I would find when I came in here today. And it's *so much* better. Now, this place has the beginnings of a real art gallery. A place someone cares about enough to pour their heart and soul into the walls." He looked around, evaluating the space once more. "Where would you put the tribe's items?" he asked, seeking her opinion before he influenced it with his own.

Laura moved forward into the center of the room, confidently. "I thought, maybe, if you liked what I'd already done, I could do a mural on the upper portion of that wall…" She pointed to the long wall at a ninety degree angle to where the cash register would be. "I'd like to do it in pale greens and browns. Forest tones, but grayed out a bit on the taupe side, so everything blends on all the walls. I want that wall to look like the forest around here. Like the tribal lands where the artisans live."

"I love that idea," Gus told her. "And what about the rest?"

"Well…" She spun around to face the wall on the other side of the cash register, on the other side of the door that led to the back. "If you're okay with it, I thought maybe I'd depict a grove of giant sequoia here, again using that taupe color palette mixed with forest colors. And walking through the trees, I thought I'd put a spirit bear."

"You want to do a portrait of me?" Gus was floored.

"You know, I've never seen your beast, but the elders seemed to like having you around," she teased him lightly, warming his heart. She turned to the far wall. The one with the door leading to the hallway and the rest of the building. "And over there, I thought I'd do something related to the cove and the water. You said the two galleries in the back will be run by mer and have sea-themed items. I thought that would be a good segue."

"It's brilliant," Gus enthused. "I want you to do all of that, and I will definitely add a bonus to your pay for it. If I had to hire an artist to do murals like this, it would cost a pretty penny, I can tell you. I don't mind paying for the value you're adding to the place. It's only fair."

She shook her head. "You've already been so generous with me. I really don't—"

"Yes, you do," Gus interrupted her. "Don't argue," he chastised her gently. "I'll be by tomorrow with some paints for you to choose from and some brushes, if you want to try

it the more traditional way, though if you want to finger paint
so it all matches, that's your call."

True to his word, Gus brought an array of paint and
supplies by the shop the next morning. Laura had started at
sunrise, prepping the wall she hoped to work on that day by
painting it completely one color, using the big roller. She
made it neat and did the trim in a glossy white that she found
among the other paints. She was halfway through treating the
door-side wall to the same when Gus walked in around nine
a.m., carrying a large box that was full of paint and brushes
and other things.

He showed her what he'd brought, and they talked for a
little while, but she was too eager to get started and shooed
him out after a half hour, with her thanks for bringing the
materials. He promised to return that afternoon with
groceries for her apartment. There had been a box of cereal
in her cupboard and a jug of milk in the fridge when she
moved in—Gus had to have put them there sometime
between showing her the place and bringing her there to
move in—so she'd been able to have breakfast.

Marilee had already promised to spend her lunch break
with Laura. She would bring sandwiches from the bakery, and
they were going to have a picnic on the wide porch of Spirit
Bear House. There were already a couple of chairs out there
and a bench or two with a small table. Gus had really thought
of everything to make the place inviting.

Laura had agreed to accept the groceries Gus promised
because she really did need them, and she figured he could
take the expense out of her pay. She'd insisted on that, and
he'd reluctantly agreed. Now, she just had to make sure he
did it. He was such a giving soul, she knew she'd have to keep
after him or he'd just give her everything for free. That was
hardly fair to him.

She'd accept help, while she needed it. She wasn't stupid
or stupidly proud. But, as soon as she could pay her own way,
she had decided she was going to pay all those who had

helped her back, with interest, if it took her ten years to do it.

Laura had made a good start on the second mural when Marilee arrived with lunch. Laura ducked into the back room, which had an attached lavatory, and washed up quickly, then joined Marilee on the porch, where she'd already started taking food out of the bag she'd brought with her.

"Those murals are amazing, Mom," Marilee said.

Laura had to catch her breath. Marilee was starting to get used to calling her Mom, but to Laura, it was a new and emotional experience. It had been so long she'd been without her child. Marilee had grown into a beautiful young woman over the twenty years in which Laura had been held captive. It was a miracle they'd been reunited, and Laura was still adjusting. Every time Marilee called her Mom or Mama, it made her heart clench in the best possible way.

"Thank you," Laura replied, accepting both the compliment and a paper-wrapped sandwich.

"I didn't know you were an artist," Marilee went on as she opened her own sandwich and popped the top on a soda can.

"I'm not really an artist. I've never done a big mural like this before, to be honest," Laura admitted. "I wasn't sure that first one was going to come out the way it did, but it was fun, and it worked." She shrugged as if it didn't matter, but secretly, she was very pleased with herself. She'd been raised to be modest, though, so she didn't wallow in her pride.

"When the others see what you've done, they're going to want you to paint their places, too," Marilee told her. "I can almost guarantee it."

Laura didn't answer because she'd just taken a huge bite of her sandwich. That bowl of cereal hadn't gone too far that morning, and she was hungrier than she realized.

"You know, everyone is preparing for a tourist season that's going to start in a few weeks. You should do some small paintings to sell. I bet they'd go like hotcakes," Marilee went on.

"Gus said something similar. I've been carving again." Laura dug into her pants pocket for the mostly-finished antler piece she'd been working on during odd moments. "This one is for Justin—the man who gave me the antlers to work with—but there's a lot more, and if Gus thinks it's good enough, I'll put some of that up for sale, maybe." She shrugged again. "I don't know who might buy this sort of thing, but you never know."

"Are you kidding?" Marilee took the carved piece in her hands and examined it closely. "Mom, this is gorgeous! How did you learn to do this?"

"There's not a lot to do in the winter up north, honey," she said, shaking her head and smiling. "After doing what you have to do to survive...when all those chores are done...carving is a good, quiet, peaceful activity to fill the hours. A lot of people carved things out of bone, and the really good carvers were given the prized walrus tusks. I got a few of those back in the day," she admitted, trying not to sound too boastful.

"I bet," Marilee said, still looking at the carving Laura had almost finished. "I don't think I'd have the patience to do something like this, but you should teach somebody. This is a skill that should be passed on."

"I hadn't thought about that, but I suppose, if anyone wants to learn, I'd be willing to teach. Carving is fun, though you have to be careful." Laura raised her left hand on which the little finger sported a bandage she'd found in the apartment's medicine chest. She'd gouged her finger but good, last night, and it still needed a bit more healing, even with her shifter constitution.

"Ouch. Is it okay?" Marilee asked, frowning.

"Yeah, it's fine now, but it bled like the dickens last night. I zigged when I should have zagged. I guess it's been too long since I last carved, and I got a bit over-confident," Laura admitted.

"Well, you know the doctor. If you need him to look at it, you should go over to the clinic," Marilee advised.

"I will if it doesn't heal up today," Laura promised.

They talked about the gallery and Laura's plans for the

other walls. She told Marilee about the name Gus had chosen and was delighted by her daughter's response. She not only didn't mind, but she loved the idea that the place would be called the White Wolf Gallery. Since Marilee was a white wolf too, if she hadn't liked it, Laura would have asked Gus to reconsider.

Laura broached the subject of the newlyweds possibly taking one of the empty apartments, and Marilee was very excited about the idea. She wasn't sure when, but if Marilee had anything to say about it, they'd be moving in across the hall sooner, rather than later.

When Marilee had to go back to work, Laura went back inside and lost herself in her painting once more. A little smile stayed on her face throughout the afternoon. Not only had she spent a pleasant hour with her beloved daughter, but as they'd sat on the porch, everyone who'd passed by had waved or called out a hello. Grizzly Cove was a marvel. The people were friendly and welcoming, even to two white wolves in a veritable sea of bears.

Throughout the afternoon, Laura heard the occasional noise from the people moving into the back galleries, but she hadn't yet met them. Every time she'd peeked out the door of what she was coming to think of as *her* shop, there was nobody in sight, and when she heard faint noises, she was usually so wrapped up in her painting that it barely registered.

Sometime in the late afternoon, a gentle knock sounded on the glass door to the gallery. Laura turned to find a stunning woman outside, smiling at her. Laura wiped her hands on a rag and went to answer the door, smiling tentatively at the woman she did not know.

"Hello, I'm Nansee. Just thought I'd introduce myself. Gus said something about you being mother hen for the building from now on, am I right?" She extended her hand, and Laura took it for a quick shake. She felt power from the other woman and noted her sea-foam blue aura. This was a woman of considerable strength, but she seemed friendly enough.

"I'm Laura. Gus described my job to me as *den mother*, but I guess it amounts to the same thing," Laura said, shrugging.

Nansee tilted her head. "His phrase is more appropriate, though. Forgive me. And welcome to the cove. I'll be in and out helping my friends set up their shops, but I wanted to stop by and introduce myself."

"That's very kind of you," Laura replied politely. "Would you like to come in? I'm just painting, and it's a bit of a mess, but if there's anything I can help you with for your friends…" She let the sentence trail off as she opened the door wider and stepped back.

CHAPTER 6

Nansee didn't say anything immediately, but did walk into the gallery, looking all around. She seemed to be taking in the finished mural of the white wolf on the wall next to the back door, then she turned her full attention to the mural Laura had been working on most of the day. It wasn't finished yet, but it was definitely starting to look like something.

"I thought so," Nansee said, inexplicably, then turned her gaze to Laura. "I could see a little through the glass at the front, but the murals you're painting are just stunning, Laura. You're very talented."

Laura fought off the blush she felt forming but tilted her head in a respectful acknowledgment of the compliment. "I've never done anything this large before, but it's fun."

"It's gorgeous, is what it is," Nansee enthused. "When you're done here, do you think you could take a look at what my friends are doing and maybe give them a few pointers?"

"Um." Laura was surprised by the request but pleased. "I'd be happy to," she finally said.

"I hope you're going to exhibit some of your own work here for sale, besides just decorating the place," Nansee went on.

"Gus mentioned the possibility," Laura replied, "but I don't have anything ready. This is the first painting I've done in decades, and I've only just started carving again."

"Carving?" Nansee looked truly interested, so Laura reached into her pocket for the piece she was doing for Justin and handed it to Nansee.

"Oh, my. This is lovely," Nansee said almost at once. "My people have a long tradition of carving, but mostly in shell or the teeth and tusks of large sea creatures."

"Where I come from, the hunters occasionally bring down aged walrus, when there is great need, and the tusks are prized. I was given several to carve when I was young," Laura admitted.

"I can see why. You're very good. If you want any materials from the sea, I could arrange to get you some. There are some particularly pretty shells, but you have to carve them wet. Apparently, the dust can be bad for you to breathe." Nansee handed the carving back to Laura.

"Oh, that sounds interesting. I always used to enjoy trying new materials. I played a little with wood when my mate and I moved south to Quebec, but that was many years ago, and I wasn't there for very long," she admitted.

"I'll bring you some things to try next time I come by," Nansee said with a decisive finality. "I'm glad to finally meet you and hope I will see you again soon."

"Likewise," Laura replied as she escorted the mer woman back to the door.

Nansee left, and Laura returned to her mural, working on it until Gus arrived sometime around six with bags of groceries in his arms. He tapped on the door, and she realized she'd been so lost in the work, she hadn't noticed the passage of time. It was getting dark out. Time to quit for the day. The mural would be finished tomorrow, she thought. All in all, it had been a good effort that day. She went to the door and met Gus, closing up the gallery and shutting off the lights.

"You work too hard," Gus said by way of greeting.

She waved him down. "Painting isn't work. That was the most fun I've had in a long time," she insisted.

"Be that as it may, we should probably establish some

ground rules—including how many hours you work in a day. I'm not a slave driver. You do get to have a life outside of work, you know." He was smiling, but she sensed he was concerned, so she gave in gracefully.

"We should probably figure out the gallery hours. I could paint a little sign for the window, to show when we're open," she volunteered.

"That would be very nice," Gus commented as he followed her up the stairs toward the apartments. "In fact, I've got some things in the back of my truck for you. Flat items of various materials—wood, slate, the more traditional canvas, and the like—that I'll bring up next. Just in case you wanted to try to make a few things to sell. You could pick out something of the right size from there for the sign, if you like."

She opened the door to her new apartment, and they went in, dumping the bags on the kitchen counter. Gus turned right back around and left with the promise to be back in a minute, with a second load.

Laura started unpacking the bags and found that he'd brought a variety of fresh fish and meat, as well as some vegetables and fruits. She set right to work cooking. She could at least feed him from the bounty he'd provided. Soon, if she was able to sell some of the creations she had yet to make, she would be able to buy her own supplies. She'd also pay Gus back for being so incredibly generous toward her. She had a definite soft spot for the guy. He'd been so nice.

Not only that, but he was handsome as sin, and didn't seem to be aware of it. She liked that about him. He was unconsciously sexy.

She was surprised by her own thoughts. It had been so long since her mate had died. She'd thought that was a true mating because she'd had a child of the union. Shifter lore said it was nearly impossible to get pregnant with someone who wasn't your true mate, but ever since awakening in Grizzly Cove and feeling this undeniable attraction to Gus, she was questioning her prior beliefs. Had Roger really been

Laura's true mate? Or had she fallen for the first handsome mage who came her way and wanted to believe it so much, she'd taken her pregnancy as proof?

It had been so long ago. She couldn't be sure now. But she was certain of the way Gus drew her. If she'd lost her true mate, it shouldn't be like that. At least, she didn't think it should. All the legends said there was only one true mate for every shifter, and if that mate was lost, it was impossible to feel such feelings for anyone else.

But what if Roger hadn't been Laura's true mate? What if getting pregnant with Marilee had been one of those rare exceptions to the rule? Or, worse yet, what if Roger had somehow used his magical skills to cause the pregnancy?

Dark clouds gathered in her soul at the mere thought of such manipulation. If he'd been able to do that, what else had he been capable of? It pained her to think that way. She'd loved him. She'd trusted him. She'd followed him to Quebec over the objections of her family. And she'd been on the run ever since.

Well, running first, then captured, then captive, and now, hiding out in the protection of Grizzly Cove. It had been a hell of a couple of decades.

Still, the niggling doubts plagued her, even as she began to cook a meal to share with Gus. What if the move to Quebec had been part of some nefarious plan to separate her from her Pack? It had certainly worked. Without them to back her up, she'd become easy prey.

And how had her mate found that mage in Quebec who was supposed to teach him in the first place? She hadn't asked too many questions back in the day, but the lack of information was truly bothering her now. How could her mate have made such a terrible mistake as to sign on as apprentice to a mage who was following an evil path? Wouldn't he have known that *before* he agreed to study with the man? And, if he did, what did that mean about his intentions? Had her mate been planning to turn to evil?

Had he mated with her under false pretenses? Had he

lured her away from her family, gotten her pregnant, taken her all the way to Quebec and then…what? Had he planned to steal her power like the other mages tried to do? Had he been outsmarted by mages more sneaky than himself?

She hated these suspicions, but she'd had a long time to consider what had happened way back then while she'd been held captive. Why had he never fought for her? Why had she had to flee on her own, so soon after giving birth to Marilee? Why had they waited to hunt her until after the baby was born? Had they wanted Marilee, to subvert her to their evil purposes?

She didn't want to believe it, but that sickening thought made the most sense. Otherwise, she would've been attacked while she was pregnant and even more vulnerable. As it had happened, she'd healed enough to run for it when they came, and she'd been able to find sanctuary for her baby before she was captured, where the evil ones had never found her.

Laura felt something like a knot at the center of her being beginning to tug. It was an uncomfortable sensation, like something coming awake that didn't want to be disturbed. She didn't know what it was, but it seemed these thoughts about her mate had started it. It felt like something magical that was blocked, trying to unblock itself. The process felt almost…itchy, even to the point of feeling painful. She didn't like it. She tried to push the feeling away and succeeded for the most part as she concentrated on preparing the food.

Gus came back in the open door then, stopping her whirling thoughts completely. He had a calming effect on her that really made a difference. Gus held another bag of groceries in one hand, and a box rested on his other arm. The box was filled with flat items standing on end of different sizes, but most were smallish, no bigger than twelve inches in any one direction. Things for her to paint. Her eyes lit up. She couldn't wait to see what he'd brought.

She barely noticed that the itchy feeling dissipated completely.

Gus kept up a lively conversation all throughout dinner, making Laura laugh at the stories he told her about some of the funnier antics he and the other men of Grizzly Cove had gotten up to as soldiers. He didn't share anything scary or secret about his missions, but the travel stories were amusing enough. Especially when he told her about the time the entire unit was supposed to travel on camels.

"Even if the camels had never scented a bear in their lives, they certainly knew we were predators. They weren't going anywhere with us. No, sir," Gus told her, grinning as he remembered it. "We ended up walking because nothing mechanical could get over that sand, and if we flew in, we'd have ruined the whole mission. My feet hurt for days. I had blisters on top of blisters. All of us did. That sand got everywhere. It was brutal."

She sympathized, though she'd never seen a desert, herself. The only sand she knew was the wet stuff down by the water. She couldn't really imagine a place where dry sand blew around like snow in a blizzard. It sounded so foreign.

"Now," Gus said, getting up to get a sealed envelope out of his jacket pocket. When he returned to the table, he put the envelope down in front of Laura. "This is for doing the murals. Don't open it now, and don't try to give it back. It's only fair. There's a bit of money in there. Not, probably, the true worth of your work, but it's what I can afford, right now, while all my ready cash is tied up in this project."

She hadn't realized he was strained for cash. That made her feel even worse about accepting all the generosity he'd shown her so far.

"If you need money, you don't have to give me this. You've already been incredibly generous."

He held up his hands, palms outward, to stop her. "No. Wait. That came out wrong. I meant to say that your art is worth ten times what's in that envelope, but I don't have it on hand, right now. I'm not a poor man. I saved up while we were all in the service. But I did sort of sink all my savings into this project, hoping to do some good for the town, and also increase my investment at the same time. That just means I'm a little low on funds until the building starts earning. I definitely want you to have this money. You deserve that, and more."

She tried to protest again, but he was having none of it. She accepted, in the end, with profuse thanks, but he waved them away. He insisted that the value she had already added to his building was well worth it, and she let the matter drop because she wasn't all that comfortable with praise. It had been so long since anybody had complimented her, she found she didn't know how to take it now. She'd have to work on that.

They talked about setting up the shop after dinner, and Gus promised to come by tomorrow afternoon to go over plans for putting out merchandise in the gallery. The opening date was drawing closer, but they still had a little less than two weeks to get everything set. He left her with a kiss on the cheek, and she tried not to feel disappointed.

Once again, she wondered if she'd really been mated all those years ago. If so, then why was she yearning for Gus's kiss like this? It didn't make sense.

She put away her questions and dug into the art supplies. First, she wanted to finish the antler piece for Justin. She wanted to repay him for his gift of the antler pieces with the gift of her carving, but she had to finish it first.

Right before she went to sleep that night, she opened the envelope and found two hundred dollars inside. She was rich! She decided, then and there, that tomorrow morning, she would start by paying back some of the folks who had provided food and lodging for her while she'd had no way to repay them. That thought firmly in mind, she slept.

The next morning, after eating breakfast in her own apartment from the groceries Gus had brought the night before, Laura went out on a mission. She was going to pay folks back, but everywhere she went, it was the same story. They wouldn't let her.

Stunned by the generosity of the townspeople, Laura was on the verge of tears most of the morning. Good tears. Happy tears. Tears of love for the amazing people of Grizzly Cove. Gus wasn't the only kind heart in this town of former soldiers and the occasional mer. She was fascinated by the way these people interacted with each other, and especially with her.

When she went into the bakery and tried to pay the sisters who owned it back for all the free meals they'd provided for her in the past days, they wouldn't hear of it. They finally relented and said she could pay for her sandwiches from here on out, but what was done, was done, as far as they were concerned, and there was no debt.

Laura decided she would have to get crafty in order to figure out how to repay these generous souls for their kindness. They seemed to like her art, so she decided she would do pieces for everyone who had helped her. The list was long, but at least now, she had money to buy more paint and supplies. All it would take was a bit of her time to decide on the best thing she could make for each person. She was already brimming with ideas.

When she went back to the gallery to work on the walls after lunch with Marilee, Laura made occasional notes on the single pad of paper she'd found in the back room about the other projects she would make for the people of the town. By the time she finished the mural on the tribe's wall, as she had come to think of it, she had a long list of projects she would be working on over the next few weeks for everybody. She would be busy, indeed.

Towards quitting time, Gus came into the gallery, carrying a couple of chairs, which he put down against the blank wall.

"These are for the back room," he said, by way of greeting. "I have a padded stool for out here in the back of my truck. I'll be right back," he told her. True to his word, a minute later, he returned with a comfy-looking stool in one hand and a bag in the other. He put the stool behind the counter and laid the bag on top. "I brought pricing paraphernalia. Stickers and pens and things we'll probably need. I built a drawer in here for this kind of stuff." He opened the small drawer under the counter and dumped the contents of the bag inside while Laura gasped.

"You're making a mess," she told him, laughing as he did.

"Maybe, but it got you to smile, so it was worth it," he replied, shooting her a wink that melted her knees. He was devastating when he was in a silly mood. When he finished with that, he leaned against the counter and looked at the wall she'd been working on. "That's really coming along. Is it done now?"

"Can't you tell?" she asked, grinning.

He came out from behind the counter and stood facing the new mural. "One learns never to rush an artist. As it is, you work really fast. Some people would take a week to do one small corner, and you did the whole thing in a day or two." He peered at her. "It is finished now, right?"

She nodded. "It's finished. I'm going to start on the next one tomorrow."

"Good," he told her, smiling wide as he returned his gaze to the finished mural, "because this is gorgeous. I can't wait to see what you do next." He stepped closer, examining the paint. "Will this be dry by tomorrow?"

"It's probably dry now. I used acrylic paints. They don't take long to dry," she told him.

"You didn't use the cans?" He looked surprised.

"I did, but only for the big parts," she clarified. "When nobody in town would take my money to pay them back, I decided to go shopping, and I bought a few tubes of acrylic paint at the shop down the way."

Gus nodded, a pleased expression on his face. "I figured nobody would take your cash. Glad they didn't." He looked over at the counter where her supplies were laid out on a drop cloth. "Still, you shouldn't have to pay for supplies to decorate this place. That's my responsibility. What do I owe you?"

"Oh, no," she said, fending him off with outstretched

palms. "You've given me enough. I won't let you reimburse me for a few dabs of paint. Besides, I needed the supplies for my own work anyway. I'm making things to give the folks who helped me when I needed it."

"You are?" Gus stopped himself. "Of course you are. Honey, you don't have to. Everyone here helps those who need it. All we expect is that you'll do the same for someone else someday."

"I see that, but I want to do a little more. People seem to like what I make, so I thought I'd make some gifts to give the people that have helped me, since they won't take my money." She shrugged. This was important to her, and she wouldn't be talked out of it.

"All right," Gus said softly. "I won't argue. But I hope you're making some things to sell in the shop, as well."

"When I have time," she answered quietly, "I will." She turned back to examine the wall and see if there were any obvious wet spots. "Why does this need to be dry? What do you have in mind?" she asked him.

CHAPTER 7

"I thought I'd bring in some of the display furniture and maybe start stocking the back room, tomorrow," he said. "We could start setting up the merchandise the tribe gave us over the next day or two, if you're game, but I don't want to interfere with your painting, and it's probably best to wait until the area is clear before we bring out the goods. I'd hate to get paint on anything important."

"That sounds good. I'll do the smaller mural on the other half of the back wall tomorrow. That's going to be the one with the giant sequoias. Once that's dry, the whole back of the shop and this wall will be ready to go. I'm going to do something sea-like in the space by the door. I just have to figure out what we're putting on that other wall and maybe something around the display window, though there isn't a lot of room with all the glass. The biggest mural—this one—is done, so the rest will be easier." She contemplated the wall space on the other side of the counter along the back wall. "You know, I could probably get a good start on this tonight, and that way, I could finish it in the morning, and we could start putting out merchandise on this side of the store tomorrow afternoon. What do you think?" She turned to Gus, enthusiasm making her almost giddy.

"I think you should probably stop for dinner, at some

point, but if you really want to, go for it. Still, I don't want you pushing yourself too hard. It wasn't that long ago, you were still recovering," he reminded her gently.

"Honestly, I love painting. I never knew how much I'd enjoy it, but I do. I was just going to go upstairs and work on my carving, anyway, so whether I do this down here or that upstairs, I'd still be up for a while, working on something. This is more important, at the moment, so I should do this first," she reasoned.

"All right," Gus reluctantly agreed. "But I'm going to go out and get dinner for you. We can eat upstairs or down here. Whichever you prefer. But we are going to eat." He gave her a mock stern look, and she nodded solemnly, though she couldn't help the smile on her face.

Gus came over and placed a gentle kiss on her forehead. "Don't work too hard. I'll be back in a couple of hours, okay?"

She nodded again, unable to speak because she was afraid her voice would come out too whispery, betraying how much his kiss—even a chaste one—affected her. She watched him go with longing in every fiber of her being. She wanted to call him back and kiss him properly, but she didn't dare. He was a holy man, on the shaman's path, and she was damaged goods. A woman who didn't even know now whether or not she'd really been mated.

Her world had been rocked by those thoughts, and now, she was a little lost. She needed to figure herself out before she could drag anyone else into the mess that was currently her life. That was her intention, at any rate. She had to be strong and not succumb to the desire that grew stronger every time she saw Gus.

A pang of...something...not good...hit her, and she grabbed for the edge of the counter to steady herself. Something was wrong. She didn't know what, but something wasn't right inside her. She shook her head, hoping to clear the haze of red that had come over her vision. She blinked hard, and it finally dissipated. Damn. Whatever this was, it was growing. Slowly, but growing.

Laura had a lot to figure out. But, first, she had a mural to paint. That thought firmly in mind, she began applying paint to the wall where she would put her giant sequoia. And, if she could convince Gus to shift for her, she'd do a portrait of the man, who was at the center of most of her thoughts, in among the trees.

A little over two hours later, Gus returned to the building he'd built on spec to find Laura laying down the base of a new mural. This one was going to the right of the area he'd built for the cash register, and she'd started with the suggestion of massive giant sequoia trees, though the color palette still had a muted feel to it that matched the other work she'd done so far.

She turned when he opened the door to the gallery, and there was a look of welcome on her face that punched him in the gut, in a good way. He'd never had such a strong response to any woman, and he had to wonder what was going on. She'd lost her mate. Neither one of them should be susceptible to this powerful attraction. At least, he didn't think it should work like that. His inner bear should know that she had lost the love of her life and feel compassion, not just...*passion*.

It seemed like all the normal rules didn't apply with Laura, though.

"That was quick," she told him, still smiling. "Whatever that is, it smells delicious."

"I was gone over two hours. I was afraid you'd be starving by now." He hefted the big shopping bag full of food onto the counter.

She laughed. "I guess I got lost in the painting."

"Where do you want to eat? Down here or upstairs?" he asked, amenable to either location. It was totally up to her.

"Upstairs is probably better. I should stop now, in any case. I want this all to dry thoroughly before I add the next layers." He wasn't sure what she meant, but it sounded like she had a definite vision for how her murals would come together. He wouldn't interfere with that. Her art was too gorgeous to stifle in any way.

"Great. Lead the way, ma'am," he said, lifting the bag again, and gesturing for her to go first.

"I'll just bring these brushes with me and wash them out in the kitchen upstairs," she explained as she took a small bucket he'd put in the box he'd dropped off earlier with supplies. It had a few inches of water in it and several paintbrushes of various sizes sticking out of the top.

He was pleased to see she'd used the things he'd brought. Somehow, it made him feel like a good provider, or something. Weird. His inner bear—usually so at peace with the world and kind of a mystical asshole, sometimes, felt smug. That was new. His bear spirit had never been smug with anyone, but it felt that way now, as if it knew something his human half didn't, and was secretly amused by it all. Furry jackass, his human mind thought at the other side of his being. The bear just chuckled inside him.

Most shifters had a small separation between their beast side and their human side, but Gus's was a little more pronounced than others because his bear was a mystic as well as being more magical than most bears. Which was saying a lot, since bears were among the most magical of all shifters.

Of course, there were a few other shifters that outclassed bears in magical terms, but they were incredibly rare. Snowcats. Dragons. Those sorts of mythical shifters, like phoenixes—which were now rumored to exist. Hell, if Gus hadn't already met a dragon shifter, he wouldn't believe they were real either. Those kinds of shifters had all sorts of magic that even bears couldn't match, though Gus was probably a little closer to that level than his friends in Grizzly Cove, since he was a spirit bear, which had complications of its own.

He'd been born this way. It wasn't something he'd asked for. It just was what he was. He'd had this old, wise spirit inside him that occasionally chuckled at the foibles of his human half. He hadn't really started to get in synch with his bear half until he'd started following the shaman's path. Only then had his bear side been truly pleased with his human side and started cooperating more fully. It was a weird separation that most other shifters wouldn't really comprehend.

He told his bear to shut up as he followed Laura up the stairs toward the apartment. He tried and failed to ignore the delectable sway of her hips as she mounted each step. She was so unconsciously graceful, and her curves were coming back now that she was eating well again. He'd known a werewolf or two in his time, but never one as lovely and downright exotic as this Arctic wolf woman. She was lovely, inside and out...and it really came out in her painting.

A tainted soul could not paint such loveliness from a black heart.

Laura started to feel odd twinges as they made their way up to her apartment. Not good, sexy twinges, but more like something evil coming awake inside her.

No. She refused to believe any of the bullshit lies the last mage who had her had spouted. She'd been out of it for the most part, but on rare occasions, she would stir inside her own mind to watch from afar what the mage tried to do to her. When he used his magic on her, she often roused, just a little, and was able to watch from within, though she didn't look any different on the outside.

He would kick her wolf body, and she wouldn't feel the pain. Her mind was dissociated from her flesh. She knew she was bleeding. Hurt. Damaged. But she didn't feel any of it. Not until she'd awakened on the stone slab in the center of the sacred circle.

The power of that place had held her together. It had helped reunite her wandering spirit with her abused mortal body. She'd thought that had been the worst of it, but at odd moments, as she healed, she had started to remember things the *Venifucus* mages had said over the years. She didn't remember all of it, yet. She wasn't sure she *wanted* to remember any of it, but she was pretty sure it was important to know just how much damage they had done to her spirit...magically.

For, while she'd mentally fled to the fey realm, her body remained locked in the mortal realm. In their control. Although most of her consciousness was elsewhere, she could not break the tie between body and mind completely. That would have meant certain death, and she'd wanted to live. She hadn't been brave enough to end her own existence in such a way. She'd had a tiny flicker of hope...somehow...all along. A petite flame of rebellion against what had happened to her and a miniscule wish that—somehow, someday, some way—she would find her daughter again.

That wish had come true, and Laura was overjoyed to be here, in Grizzly Cove, knowing her baby was happy and mated to a wonderful man who would always take care of her as she would him. She felt supremely blessed to be able to see her baby girl every day and talk about all the things they'd missed and all the happy times that were yet to come for them as a family. A small family but, hopefully, a growing one. Marilee was mated now, after all. Perhaps Laura would be a grandmother someday. The thought made her smile.

But the problems of the past weren't going to go away so easily. As she remembered odd snatches of conversation between the mages and felt these sinister stirrings inside her core, she wondered...and worried. Had they done something to her that would make her dangerous to her daughter, or others, or to the town, in general? She didn't know, but she was maintaining a vigilant stance, watching her own power levels and noting any flares or shifts in energy.

Like right now, as Gus went into the dining area and placed the bag of food on the table. She felt something almost painful twisting inside her. Not physically, but on the plane where magic existed. Something was waking up. Stirring. Watching... Hating.

Fear coursed through her for a split second, and she

opened her mouth to warn Gus, and then, suddenly…it was gone. Had she imagined it? Was it all a product of the anxiety that seemed to be building in her very bones?

Laura shook her head and went to the table to help Gus set out the boxes of hot, delicious-smelling food. The odd feeling was gone for now. If it came back, she'd talk to him about it. Maybe Gus could help her…if she wasn't imagining it. She just couldn't be sure. Not yet, at any rate.

The pieces of conversation she'd recalled were too fragmented, and the feeling she'd experienced up to now had been too vague. There'd been that one flash of violent hatred, but it had gone poof. Disappeared so fast, she wasn't even sure if what she'd felt had been real, or some strange figment of her overactive imagination. Was she jumping at shadows? Or was there really something to be worried about?

She would worry, regardless. Anxiety seemed to be her near-constant companion lately. But she'd been through a lot. She couldn't expect for everything to be back to normal so soon after being freed. She might have issues for years to come, and the worst of it probably hadn't quite hit her yet. She would watch and wait. She would continue her vigilance, and if something came of it, she knew to ask for help. She didn't want to hurt anyone—herself or others. She'd seek help before it became an issue. That was her plan, at least.

She put all that behind her for the moment and sat down to a lovely meal with Gus. He was a witty companion, and she enjoyed his steady, stable, calming company.

Of course, he was also kind of exciting to be around, too. For one thing, he was sexy as all get out. He had those handsome eyes and chiseled cheeks. She wondered what his bear form looked like. She'd love to see it, but maybe not now. No, as dinner was consumed and dessert made an appearance, she started thinking about how much she'd rather see his naked human form right about now.

It had been so long since she'd been with a man. She hadn't thought she'd ever find another man attractive after committing her heart to her handsome mage, but Gus was doing things to her, without even trying. He was creating a yearning she had never expected to feel again. A wanting. A desire.

Damn.

"Are you all right, Laura?" Gus asked gently as they sat on the couch and sipped coffee after their meal. She hadn't wanted the night to end, so she'd offered to make coffee, and he'd accepted.

"I'm sorry," she apologized immediately, knowing he'd caught her mind wandering. She blushed a little at the thoughts that had been going through her very naughty mind. "Gus..." she began hesitantly, "...you're a shaman. You counsel people, right? About magical things, right?"

He nodded, putting his coffee cup down on the saucer on the low table in front of the couch. His brows furrowed as he looked at her. "I do," he confirmed. "Do you have something you want to talk about with me, Laura?"

She set her cup down, too, keeping her eyes downcast. She didn't think she could discuss this if she looked at him. He was just too attractive.

"I've been worried about a few things. In particular, I'm concerned that maybe my mating with Roger wasn't...real." There. She'd said it aloud, and the earth hadn't shattered. She dared to peek up at Gus, and he had a gentle expression on his calm face. He looked like he genuinely wanted to help, and it gave her courage.

"What makes you say that?" he asked in a quiet voice.

"Well, I was so in love with him, and when I conceived Marilee, I assumed that was proof positive that Roger and I were true mates. I mean, isn't that how it works? Shifters aren't usually all that fertile with those not destined for them by the Goddess, right?"

"That is the conventional wisdom," Gus said in deliberate tones that didn't really tell her what he thought about it. "Of course, you're not completely shifter in your heritage. I don't know how things work for fey. Maybe that influence changes things for your line. Was there ever any discussion of that in your family?" he asked.

Laura shook her head. "My family objected to my leaving with Roger for the south, but I thought that was because they just didn't want me to go. Our Pack was very close. It was hard to leave them."

"And, yet, you did," Gus mused.

"Roger was my mate, and I was pregnant. I wanted to be with him," she said immediately.

"But now, you're wondering if the mating was real," Gus reminded her. "Tell me. What makes you question it?"

How could she tell Gus that she was concerned because she was attracted to *him*? No. She couldn't do that. But what could she say? She hesitated before answering.

"I don't feel the way I would expect to feel if I had lost a true mate," she said. "It's not the soul-deep wound I would have expected. Then again, a lot of time has passed, but I always thought that wouldn't matter. A true mate is for life. That's what everyone says."

"What else?" he asked, not letting her off the hook.

Dare she tell him more? She had, after all, been the one to ask for his counsel. She should at least give him some of the truth, if not all of it, so he could do as she asked and give the best advice possible. Otherwise, she would be short-changing them both.

"I feel...things...when I'm around you, Gus. Things I probably shouldn't be feeling if Roger had been my true mate." She was both shocked and amazed that she'd found the nerve to tell him that flat out. Then again, she'd always been a bold woman when she was sure of her subject matter. It was only now, after twenty years of the world going on without her, that she found herself being hesitant about things because she was so far behind everyone else.

Gus moved closer on the couch, taking her hand in his. "I feel things around you, too, Laura. Things that go way beyond what they should for a woman who'd already been mated to someone else. For what it's worth, I feel instinctively that you were never truly mated to Roger. You may have had a child with him, but that's not always absolute proof. For one thing, your fey blood might've had an influence, and for another—and forgive me for saying this— he *was* a mage. He could've done something…" Gus let his words trail off, but Laura knew exactly what he meant.

"I'm sorry to admit that the thought had crossed my mind," she told him, squeezing his hand gently. "I can see now, that my younger self was a bit of a headstrong fool, in love for the first time and extremely stupid about the entire situation. No wonder my family objected."

"They loved you," he said gently, drawing closer. "I can see why. You're an easy woman to admire."

CHAPTER 8

Is it getting hot in here? It sure felt that way as Gus edged closer to her on the couch.

His lips found hers, and that was the end of their discussion. What started gentle soon turned tempestuous. Gentle licks of his skilled tongue soon turned into demanding thrusts, mirroring what she wanted him to do to the rest of her body…with the rest of his.

She lay back on the long couch, and he followed her down, covering her body with his. It felt so good. So warm and caring. So hot and needy.

She pushed at his clothes, not very effective as she grabbed the fabric covering his shoulders and tried to push it away, but Gus got the message. He lifted up slightly, and then, his shirt was off, and tossed across the room.

He had tanned skin and rippling muscles. Bear shifters were built on the big side, but Gus was different than the pseudo-linebackers that made up the town. He was as big as any grizzly, but he was lean and ripped, not bulky in any way. His human form was delectable, and she wanted to lick him all over.

He broke their kiss again, when he sought permission, wordlessly, to help her rid herself of her top. She didn't wait for him to do it. She tugged the offending material off over her head and let it sail across the room to follow his shirt. Then, she gasped as Gus's lips closed over her shoulder, his sharp teeth grazing her skin in a tantalizing way before he moved inward to lick and kiss her neck. He moved downward as her chin lifted up, giving him free access. Damn. That felt so good.

His skin was hot. Smooth. Perfect. She caressed him as he nibbled his way down her neck and then over her chest. Her bra was pulled aside by his eager teeth, and then, he licked her nipple, sending delicious shivers down her spine.

She lost track of time while Gus made her feel things she'd thought long forgotten. He treated her like a queen, putting her pleasure first and foremost. She might have felt a little guilty about it, but she was enjoying herself too much to do anything about it. She'd pay him back—with interest—later. She was already thinking about the naughty things she could do to show her appreciation. With any luck, she'd remember her old skills, and the man wouldn't know what hit him.

That was the last thought she remembered thinking before Gus took them both to a whole new level. He kissed his way down her torso and then rid her of her pants in a masterful motion that left her gasping. It was sudden. It was exciting. And more than a little explosive. Her desire ratcheted up another notch as he relieved her of her pants and panties, then spread her out before him like a feast.

His mouth returned to her body, and she just about lifted off the couch when his tongue touched her clit. The man knew what he was doing, and she cried out, grasping his hair in her hands as he brought her to a small completion.

It had been far too long for her. Decades. But being with Gus this way wasn't awkward in the least. In fact, the way he touched her gave her confidence. He made her feel desirable. Competent. Powerful. Never had a man made her feel quite this way, and it called into question everything that had come before in her life, but now was not a time for such deep thoughts.

No, as Gus rose above her and met her gaze with a

question in his own, there was only one thought possible. Only one answer to the question in his eyes.

"Yes," she breathed, and he smiled down at her, slowly joining his body to hers.

He slid into her with gentle motions designed to make this as easy as possible on her. She hadn't been with a man in many years, and his consideration brought a tear to her eye, even if it wasn't really necessary. Her body seemed to remember what to do readily enough, and she was more than ready for his possession.

He held her gaze throughout the joining, probably watching for any sign of distress. He was such a caring man. She could easily love him. A scary thought. The last man she'd loved had left her with many questions and her life in ruins. She wasn't sure what this next chapter of her existence would bring, but she was going to be more careful about who she trusted with her heart, this time.

But Gus really made her want to throw caution to the wind, again. For now, she'd just enjoy the moment…and the man. Never had she felt so alive. Perhaps it was because she'd been essentially comatose for so very long, but Gus's possession brought her back to the mortal world fully…forcefully…finally.

Their eyes held as he began to move. Her inner wolf came out in the low growl that issued from deep in her chest. It was a sound of approval, of play and challenge, all in one. Gus answered her beast with a rumbling tone of his own. Fuller. Deeper. Bigger. He was a bear, and her wolf knew it, but the wolf also knew *this* bear would never hurt her. *This* bear had shown her only kindness, and now, he was showing her what passion could be, all over again.

It had been so long…

Gus's movements were gentle at first as he looked deep into her eyes…into her soul. She couldn't look away. Perhaps it was his magic. Perhaps it was just the man, himself. Whatever it was, she wanted more of it. Of him.

She grasped his arms, loving the hard feel of his muscles

under the velvet of his skin. His deep brown eyes held hints of his power. Swirls of magic lit him from within to her keen sight. He was even more magical then most of the amazing bears she'd seen in this town, and the way he looked at her stole her breath, sometimes. As he moved within her, it felt like he was looking into her heart, and the focused expression on his face as he brought her to peak after peak spoke to her of care and determination to please her.

How had she gotten so lucky as to find a man like this? A lover who put her needs before his own, as he was doing, now. She cried out at the climax that hit her all at once, and still, he kept going. Powering within her, he brought her up again to the precipice, but this time, he flew over it with her, carrying them both out into the abyss where only pleasure existed. Just for the two of them.

The next morning, Gus was gone before Laura woke. She woke up, expecting to feel buyer's remorse, but instead, she just blushed when she remembered the tender way he'd made love to her all night. And it had been *all* night. Male shifters had a reputation for having more…ahem…stamina than the average male. There were various legends about the different types of shifters and their sexual proclivities and habits. After last night, she believed every last little juicy piece of gossip she'd ever heard about bear shifters.

It really was true. They could go all night long. And they were patient. A least, Gus was. He'd been patient, kind and understanding of her periodic moments of hesitation. He'd led her through them so beautifully. It had just been so long since she'd been with a man. Every touch, every caress, had told her without words that Gus understood. What a fantastic guy. And he was a hell of a lover. She found herself smiling, and her cheeks flushed with heat as she remembered some of the highlights of the night before.

She found he'd left her a note with a flower he'd gotten from somewhere. Had he gone all the way out, and come all the way back, just to leave her a flower? She smiled as she sniffed the wild rose. They must grow around here somewhere, but she hadn't seen them. She'd caught the faint scent of them a time or two while she'd been walking down the beach, but she hadn't been able to pinpoint where the scent had come from. Gus knew, apparently, just where the wild roses grew. He'd gone and picked one for her and had come back just as silently—letting her sleep—to give her a sweet surprise when she woke.

His note expressed his regret at having to leave, but he'd had an early meeting at the reservation and hadn't had the heart to wake her up, just to say goodbye. He'd gone so far as to write that he didn't think he'd have been able to leave if she'd been awake, and he'd promised to return for lunch with a fresh load of art and jewelry pieces from the artists on the res.

Laura couldn't wait until she saw him, again, but she felt a little anxious about how their reunion would go. Would he be as loving and warm as he'd been the night before, or was their liaison just another in a string for him? Male shifters were notorious for sowing their wild oats until they were blessed to find their true mate.

Laura had already had a mate, so logically, Gus couldn't be hers. Right? She had come to question the past quite a bit since meeting Gus, but she was so confused about the entire situation. She resolved to let Gus be her guide. How he acted when he came back to see her would give her the answer about how she should handle this. That decision made and a quick breakfast eaten, Laura headed down to the gallery to work on her mural until Gus reappeared.

Gus didn't arrive until mid-morning, and by that time, the mural was almost finished—except for the bear she wanted to put in walking among the redwoods. She'd insert him later, she decided. Possibly.

The thing was... She didn't want it to be just some generic bear in the woods she had created. She wanted it to be Gus. It was his building. His gallery. He should be represented in the art, somehow. But to date, she'd never seen his animal form. She could make some educated guesses, but she wanted to see the spirit bear first, before she painted him.

Gus didn't seem to notice that there was something missing from the mural. He had walked in, dropped a box on the counter and stared for a moment at the towering redwoods she'd depicted in soft shades of green, cream, and brown. A muted interpretation of reality that matched the other murals in the room, tying the whole place together.

"Magnificent," he said after a moment studying the art she'd created. He came over and put his arms around her from behind, leaning down to kiss her temple. "You're a true artist, Laura. You've captured the immenseness of those trees, and yet, also the spiritual nature of the place. I love it."

"It's not completely done yet, but this is as far as I can go, right now," she admitted. He didn't ask what else she wanted to add. He just let her statement stand without comment.

They just stood there, his big body wrapped around hers as he contemplated the mural for a long moment. Then, he sighed and seemed to come out of the trance the scene had put him into.

"Do you want to go there for lunch?" he asked.

"Go where?" She turned as he released her from his embrace.

"To the redwoods," he said, gesturing toward the mural. "There's a grove near my property, still within the boundary of the town's ward. It's safe. I like to walk up there. We could pack a picnic lunch and take an hour or two. What do you think?"

There was so much work to do to get the gallery ready, but she wanted to spend time in Gus's company. With just him, and the giant sequoia trees. She wanted that more than she could say. The real-life version of the mural she had almost finished painting. She smiled up at him.

"Let's do it."

Gus drove them to his place first. They'd already stopped in town for a hamper of food from the bakery, and the conversation on the way to his place had been casual and pleasant. He couldn't keep himself from holding Laura's hand as they drove along. Touching her had become a necessity for his inner peace.

Dangerous. He knew he was setting himself up for a very big fall, but he felt powerless against the force of the attraction he felt for Laura.

He knew, as well as any other bear, that shifters mated just once…and for life. Laura had already had a mate, though they both seemed to have their doubts about the validity of the mating. He could hope that Roger hadn't been Laura's true mate, but he also knew that wasn't likely. Shifters were usually only fertile with their true mate. Otherwise, there would be a lot more little half-shifters running around.

As it was, it was a very rare occurrence for a shifter to have a child with someone who wasn't their true mate. Marilee's very existence seemed to validate her parents' union. Of course, Marilee's father had been a mage.

In the back of Gus's mind, that small fact gave him hope. Had the mage somehow been able to influence Laura's fertility? Had he manipulated the entire situation? If so, he'd never been Laura's true mate, which left room for Gus. But it would also mean that the entire relationship had been a sham. A scam. A way to get to Laura.

It was pretty obvious that Laura had loved her mate. If he'd been deceiving her from the very beginning, he'd been a cad of the first order, and having proof of his duplicity would hurt her. Gus knew she had suspicions. But that's all they were, right now—suspicions. He didn't want to hurt her feelings by bringing up the subject, again. They had time. If his level of attraction didn't abate, then he'd have to look more deeply into her past.

As it was, for now, at least, he could let things ride and just enjoy her company. The turmoil of his thoughts was well hidden and could remain so for a while longer. And who knew? Maybe if she felt strongly about Gus, they might be able talk over her past with Roger with a minimum of pain—

though he knew, if she'd been deceived by Marilee's father, she'd be both angry and hurt. Of course, if she really had been that mage's true mate and she couldn't return Gus's feelings—then the pain would be all on Gus's side. It might be cowardly, but he decided he'd rather put off that discovery as long as possible.

They walked to the redwood grove from his place. It wasn't far, and like he'd told her, he often walked among the towering trees. It was a sacred place. A place where he came to think and just...be.

"We're near the border with the res here," he told her as they walked along in the regular-sized pines. The redwood grove wasn't far, but they'd come upon it suddenly, sneaking up on it from the forest.

"So, who owns this land?" she asked as they strolled along.

"I own some of it," Gus replied. "But not all. More than a few lots have been left vacant so the town can expand. Now, on the far side of the redwood grove, some newlyweds have moved in, and this isn't the only grove inside the town's perimeter. It's just the one closest to my place." He recognized where they were and slowed his pace deliberately. "Get ready now," he told her, almost whispering. "Do you see it?"

Laura practically tiptoed a few paces in front of him to peek through the trees, and then, she gasped. Gus smiled. She'd seen the Sentinel. That's what he called the first forest giant that signaled the presence of the grove to him. He loved how that massive trunk just seemed to loom out of the forest all of a sudden. It never failed to impress him, or the few people he'd taken along this route.

"That's *one* tree?" she asked, her gaze glued to the giant tree as her steps slowed to a stop.

Gus nodded. "One ancient tree. I call him the Sentinel because he's the first I see when I come this way, and it's like he's acting as lookout for the others. He's larger than the others, so he could very well be the progenitor of the entire grove."

"You think the tree is male?" She shot him an amused look.

Gus tilted his head. "Maybe. I'm not sure. I know trees are different. They produce both male and female parts to make the seeds for the next generations, but this particular tree is so massive and magical in its own way. It just feels right to refer to it as a living being, and in English, you have to choose between *him* or *her*. I went with *him*."

Laura shrugged after a moment's thought. "Makes sense, I guess. And he is incredibly huge. Bigger than I ever expected."

"But you painted him. The first tree in your mural. That's this tree, isn't it?"

Gus was confused. He had thought he'd recognized the branch pattern, but he wasn't sure. She might possibly have seen the Sentinel from a distance, somehow... Then again, he hadn't really been thinking. When would she have seen this tree? No time that he could think of. Something skittered along his spine—a tingly feeling he didn't like. What was going on here? Was her knowledge of this place a benevolent gift of the Mother, or was it something that had been planted in Laura's mind, by evil forces?

Thankfully, she didn't seem to notice his tension. Laura shrugged and continued to gaze upward at the Sentinel tree. "No, I was just making it up. I've never seen giant sequoia in person before. I saw photos in text books a long time ago, but I've never been among them myself."

Gus was silent as he followed her gentle footsteps closer to the tree, and the grove it heralded. He shook off his discomfort, as best he could. There was nothing to be done at this moment, and no real conclusive proof that something was amiss. He would continue to observe, of course, but he was also going to enjoy this time among the giant redwoods that he loved so much. Sharing them with Laura was special. He wouldn't let shadows of something that might, or might not, develop into a problem, ruin it.

"Oh," Laura murmured as she cautiously walked around

SPIRIT BEAR

the circumference of the massive tree and discovered what lay beyond. He could hear the awe in her voice. "There are so many of them," she whispered, as if talking too loudly would break the spell the woodlands cast over them. "They're so huge!"

Gus came up beside her as she paused at the base of the Sentinel, now on the other side of the massive tree where she could see the rest of the grove stretching into the distance. She was looking straight up, her head lolling back to take in the enormity of the tall pine.

"This is like nothing I could have expected. I think I need to re-work my mural," she said after a moment. "I got the scale all wrong."

"Really? I thought your mural was spot on," Gus said quietly, contemplating the trees as he liked to do when he came here.

Laura shook her head. "The mural isn't finished yet. There's supposed to be a bear walking among the trees, but I was picturing him way too large for the scale of the trees."

"So, just make the bear smaller," Gus said, shrugging. "The trees won't mind."

She looked at him, frowning even as she smiled. "But what if I wanted the bear to be the focal point, not the trees?"

Gus shook his head. "Very little in this world can compete with these forest giants. The bear knows this. Don't try to force something that is inevitable. These trees were here long before our people, and Goddess willing, they will be here long after."

She tilted her head, as if considering his words, but said nothing in reply.

"Follow me," he told her, moving their day along. "There's a great little spot just ahead where we can have our picnic."

85

CHAPTER 9

The picnic spot was everything Gus promised, and more. Set in the center of a triangle anchored by three of the giant sequoia, one on each point, was a sun-dappled clearing filled with tufts of grass, strewn pine needles and the occasional fern and wildflower. It was like a mini paradise.

Gus spread the picnic blanket he had brought with them in the center of the triangle. He placed the picnic basket on one corner then motioned for her to sit. She liked the feel of the earth beneath the blanket and the scents of the forest all around. When Gus opened the basket, the scents of their lunch became dominant for a while, dissipating as they ate, surrounded by nature's beauty.

When lunch had been consumed and they were both sitting comfortably on the blanket, enjoying the sounds of the forest, time seemed to slow, and each breath of the fine, fresh air became precious and filled with fairy dust. Maybe it was just the effect of the sunlight dancing through the canopy far overhead, but the small clearing in which they sat seemed even more magical than before. Laura sat while Gus reclined, leaning up on his elbows, seeming to contemplate the dappled sun on the world below.

"I love it here," he said, his deep voice flowing into the forest, a part of it. Welcome. As if he belonged here.

"I can see why," she replied. Her voice wasn't quite as in tune with the place yet, but she hoped, one day, it would be. She was fast becoming enamored of this magical place. "It's really beautiful."

Gus got to his feet and began undressing. "It's even better when your senses are completely open. Want to shift with me?" He kicked off his shoes and paused for her answer.

Laura had to try twice to get her words out past her suddenly dry mouth. She gulped and tried again. "I haven't shifted since..."

"Since finally regaining your human form," Gus completed her thought. "I suspected as much." He frowned a bit as he regarded her. "You can't keep the wolf at bay forever. She needs to be part of your recovery just as much as your human side. Don't shut her out."

"But I was trapped in her body for so long," Laura said, unable to hold his gaze. She looked down at the blanket, following the patterns of light play across its surface.

"She is a part of you. Half of you. You can't just ignore her. The wolf kept you safe for all those years. It's not fair to shut her out now," Gus said softly. Even though his words were gentle, the truth of them hit her hard.

"You don't pull any punches, do you?" She looked up at him, though she kept her head mostly down.

Gus sat again, barefoot now, taking up a position opposite her. "Look," he began, his tone still quiet. "I can never fully understand what it is you did to survive so long under such harsh conditions. You were wolf in this plane of existence, but were you also wolf in the fey realm?"

"I wasn't completely there," she told him, trying to find the words that would explain the strange in-between place to which her consciousness had fled for protection. "I could sense the fey realm, and I could sometimes sense the mortal realm through my body, but I was sort of...*between*. That's the best way I can put it. I'm not an expert on metaphysics. I just did what seemed best at the time, and thanked the Mother of All that it worked."

"Nothing wrong with that." Gus's expression, when she chanced a glance at him, held a slight frown. "So then, your consciousness was neither human nor wolf. It was just you, at your most basic, right?"

Her shoulders tensed. "Well... I'm not really sure. It was like another part of me—that fey part that had never really shone before started to brighten. The fey part seemed to know where to go. It was that part that led the way and kept the rest of my soul out of reach of the enemy. At least, that's what I think happened. Like I said, I'm no expert."

"Perhaps, at some point, we should consult an expert. Purely as an academic exercise, it would be interesting to find out if anyone else has ever used such techniques. Such knowledge might be useful to others if they find themselves in a difficult situation."

"I pray that nobody ever ends up held the way I was," Laura said at once. "But I do see your point, and I'd be interested to find out if anyone in this realm has a theory about where I was for so long." She dared greatly, about to reveal something she hadn't told anybody before. "I think... I think it changed me," she whispered. "I was more shifter than fey before. Now, it feels like all the time I spent *elsewhere* has brought the fey side of my heritage a little closer to the surface."

Gus seemed to consider her words for a long moment, then he smiled, easing her tension. "All the more reason to get back to being a shifter. Like you were before. Unafraid to take either shape that's natural to you. Your wolf needs to run, and your human side needs to trust the wolf again. She kept you safe for all that time. Trust her now, to be part of your soul, fully integrated and ready to partner your human side as it did before."

"But what about the fey part?" She really was concerned about the magic she could sense, now, that she had never sensed before.

She'd always looked the part of her fey ancestry, as had many of her relatives, but they were shifters first. The fey lineage had been diluted over time. Or so she had thought. She very much feared that her exposure to other realm had brought the fey in her out of hiding.

What that would mean for her in the long run, she had no idea. She'd always been just a shifter. A white wolf with super sparkly fur, but still, just a shifter. Now? She wasn't really sure what she was anymore.

"It was always part of you," Gus told her gently. "It's just closer to the surface now. When you needed it, it rose. Look on it as a new skill or helpful ability. Learn how to use it. Explore its boundaries. Not to do so would be a waste, and could even be potentially dangerous. If you have a power, you need to learn how to wield it responsibly. Just like you learned, as a pup, how to maneuver with your teeth and claws safely. Just like that, only a lot more magical."

She shook her head and gave a soft chuckle. "You make it all sound so easy."

"Honey, you were born the way you were for a reason. The Mother of All doesn't make mistakes. She gifted you with all the powers, skills and abilities of your heritage. It's up to you to figure out how to use them to serve Her Light." Gus stood up again, and reached down a hand to offer her help in getting up. She didn't *need* help getting up, of course. This was more a symbolic gesture, and she recognized it for what it was. "There are no shortcuts. The Lady gives us the tools, it's up to us to learn to use them to the best of our abilities. If we don't, then shame on us. The Goddess helps those who help themselves."

Laura pursed her lips and nodded slowly. "I've heard that one before." She took his hand and let him pull her up to stand in front of him.

"Let your wolf run, Laura," Gus coaxed. "Let her know she's still a valued part of you, even if other things have changed." He moved back a few paces and lifted his shirt off over his head, giving her a saucy grin. "There's no better way to experience the magic of this place than in our fur."

Laura was distracted—as she always was—when Gus took

off the rest of his clothing. Naked, he let her watch as he morphed into the most beautiful bear she had ever seen. Growing up in the arctic, she'd seen many polar bears. While Gus's fur was not brown, it wasn't the pure white of a polar bear either. It was more a soft cream…like the colors she'd chosen for her murals.

She knew immediately how she would finish the redwood scene. Gus's cream-colored fur would fit perfectly with the theme she had created. Anybody who had seen the Spirit Bear would know what her mural showed, but only those who knew Gus was the Spirit Bear would know she would be painting his portrait.

Daring greatly, she shucked her clothes and allowed the wolf to take her body. It had been so long since she'd been free to shift back and forth between her forms. She was rusty, but she found that once she became the wolf again, her fur felt familiar…and much loved. She had missed this other part of herself while she'd been human.

Fear had kept her in her human shape. Fear that, once she shifted, she'd be trapped once more in that form. It was unreasonable, she knew, but she couldn't help the way she felt. Fear was a near-constant companion. Fear that she would be recaptured. Fear that she would lose all that she had just regained. So much fear. It was a terrible companion to her every waking moment and filled many of her anxious dreams.

Only when she was with Gus did the fear recede. He kept the nightmares at bay. He made her feel safe. And, now, seeing his bear form, she could see the magic of him. The Goddess-blessed shape of his bear. Gus wasn't an ordinary man. He was a shaman. Filled with an ancient power held in reserve for when it was needed.

Laura realized, in that moment, that a lot of his friends and coworkers in Grizzly Cove probably didn't realize the extent of his power. It was deep and connected to something so immense, she could just barely sense it, but not see it in its entirety. He was an extension of the Light that shone through the universe, bringing goodness and justice to the dark places. He was a benevolent spirit dedicated to the will of the Mother of All.

Laura could actually see the strong thread of power that wound from his being, down into the earth and out into the cosmos. She'd never witnessed anything as powerful, though she recognized the pattern from the few holy people she had encountered in her lifetime. She'd known instinctually that Gus was something special, but this went well beyond her expectations.

He padded up to her in his bear form, approaching slowly so as not to scare her, but she could never be afraid of Gus. She closed the distance and sniffed at his fur, wanting to be certain of his intentions before she did anything. She'd never been this close to a bear shifter before. She didn't know if his people had some sort of protocol. She would observe and learn, and follow his lead.

At her cautious approach, he made a grunting sound and snuffled closer to her, his nose tickling her ribs. He seemed playful, so she rubbed her cheek along his side. His fur was so soft. It had a different texture than wolf fur. Softer. Finer. And he smelled different than her wolf brethren. She found the scent of his bear both alluring and dangerous. A heady combination.

When he started walking, she followed him, concentrating on him at first, rather than the scenery. After a while, though, she couldn't help but notice the energy of the grove. Every gigantic tree had an aura all its own. She could see things so much clearer in her wolf skin. Every leaf, every pine needle, every branch had a signature.

Forgetting her fear, Laura bounded ahead to investigate the next forest giant, and then the next. Before she knew it, an hour had passed as she walked among the trees, her companion a ghostly Spirit Bear.

At that point, Gus started herding her back toward the entrance to the grove, where they'd had their picnic. She was sad to see her moments of exploration come to an end, but she knew it was for the best. She had to get back to work. She had a mural to finish, and she knew just how to do it now. Her fingers itched to pick up a brush and paint.

When they reached their picnic blanket, Gus shifted first. He dressed while she watched, wanting to enjoy a few more moments in her fur before going back. She'd been afraid to shift since her rescue, and she wasn't completely sure about shifting back.

Gus dressed as he watched her. "We were getting close to the ward," he told her as he tugged on his pants and then shrugged into his shirt. "I didn't want to cross over onto tribal land, though they usually don't mind. I think it's just safer for you to stay within the ward for now."

Just like that, Laura flowed back into her human form. It had been easier than she expected. She'd thought about the things she wanted to say to Gus and how she needed to be human in order to speak with him and then…she was. Presto change-o. Huh.

She sat back and gathered her clothing, dressing only a little self-consciously. "It's okay," she told him. "I want to get back to the gallery anyway. I've got a painting to finish." She grinned as she thought about her new vision for the composition.

Gus worked in the back room while Laura painted in the front part of the gallery that afternoon. He'd picked up several boxes of wares from the res. Apparently, the artisans had been working overtime to produce items suitable for sale, and as a result, Gus had enough stock to put some in back. He worked on setting up an inventory system and entering the items into the database he'd already created. He had a plan to teach Laura how to use the computer by starting her out with just the inventory control system he'd devised. He'd made it as simple as he could, in order to encourage her.

She didn't know it yet, but once he got her comfortable with that, he had plans to introduce her to her new smart phone. He'd already purchased it, but he wouldn't spring it on her, right away. She had a lot of catching up to do as far as technology was concerned.

Gus deliberately stayed busy in the back room to give Laura space to complete her masterpiece. And it *was* a masterpiece in his estimation. She was incredibly talented, and every mural she had painted in the gallery was absolutely stunning. He didn't want to interfere with a genius at work. Few had seen the murals, yet, but he knew that once people got a good look at what she'd created here, her reputation would rise as a true artist.

As he was finishing up with his inventory, Laura surprised him by coming into the back and giving him a megawatt smile that made her eyes sparkle. She was happy. He loved seeing her that way.

"Got a minute?" she asked.

"For you, I have more than one," he answered readily. "What's up?"

"I finished the redwood mural. Want to see?" she asked, a bit shyly.

Gus got up from the chair he'd been sitting in behind the desk and joined her by the door. "Of course," he told her, putting one hand on her lower back as he escorted her into the main room. He loved touching her, and it had been far too long since he'd done so.

They went through the door, and Gus turned to look at the mural. It had been beautiful before, but now... His breath caught.

"Is that...me?" She had painted him into the redwood scene, his cream-colored coat unmistakable to those who knew of the existence of the Spirit Bear.

"Do you like it?" she asked. He could hear the tension in her tone, as if she wasn't sure how he'd react to the intensely flattering depiction she'd created of his beast half.

"Like it?" he breathed, taking in the finely detailed scene. She'd captured the scale of the giant sequoias perfectly. The bear was dwarfed by the massive trees, as he was in real life. Somehow the addition of the bear to the composition added more depth and scale to the entire thing, making it even more majestic. "Honey, you've outdone yourself. And I'm incredibly flattered that you would put me into one of your paintings." He turned to take her into his arms. "Thank you," he said, kissing her temple then her cheek. "I'm overwhelmed."

"Now, we're both on the wall," she replied in a soft voice.

He looked at the entirety of the back wall of the gallery where the two murals were separated by the doorway. Laura's white wolf was on the left, and now, Gus's bear form was on the right. She'd painted them facing each other and both in motion as if they were walking toward each other. He wondered if she'd done that on purpose, but it didn't matter. He would take it as a sign that even she thought they could meet in the middle. Gus liked that thought very much.

"How about, as a thank you for immortalizing me in your mural, I take you out to dinner?" he asked, wanting to spend more time with her.

"I'm a mess! No way," she told him, laughing and holding up her paint-stained hands. "How about we have dinner upstairs, instead?"

Oh, he liked the sound of that even better. "All right, but we're not cooking. I'm going to call Zak and get him to make us dinner to go. What would you like?"

They discussed various options for a few minutes before deciding on what he would request. Gus sent Laura upstairs to get cleaned up while he called Flambeau's and put in the order, plus a few modifications of his own.

Gus closed up the gallery and shut off the lights before heading off down the street to pick up the dinner he'd ordered. He spent a few minutes talking with John, who happened to be waiting for food as well, while Zak finalized the food orders in the kitchen. A lot of folks picked up their meals from Zak or the bakery, since they were the only two eating establishments in town, so far.

"How is it going with Laura?" John asked casually. Almost too casually. Gus knew what his friend and Alpha was really asking, and Gus was uncomfortable all over again, with the idea of spying on her.

"She's turned out to be quite the artist," Gus said.

"I'll have to come take a look. Maybe tomorrow, if my schedule allows," John replied.

"We'll be starting to set up some of the displays tomorrow. The artisans on the res really came through," Gus reported.

"That's good. Any repercussions?"

Gus knew John was talking about the tribe's new understanding that the town just to the north of the res really was populated by shapeshifters. John hadn't been thrilled by the news that the elders both knew and accepted that a town full of shifters lived nearby, but he'd shrugged it off after the initial upset.

"Nope. Everything is good. Actually, it's a bit better than it was before," Gus admitted.

"Laura's doing, you think?" John asked, one eyebrow raised in a speculative way.

"She's definitely part of it. The elders really liked her when they met her," Gus told his Alpha. "She understands the native lifestyle probably better than a lot of the folks on the res. They seem to look up to her and the more primitive survival skills she grew up learning. There's even talk of her showing some of the res kids how the Inuit do things way up north, but that'll have to wait until she can cross the ward, unless they want to come up to my backyard and do it there."

"I like the idea of building better relations with the tribe," John mused. "And I'm glad Laura's finding acceptance. I know she had a rough time finding work until you came up with your job offer."

So, John knew about that, huh? Gus wasn't surprised. John had his finger on the pulse of the town, which was his creation, after all.

Gus shrugged. "It was a good solution. I needed someone to look after my investment, and she needed a job and a place to live. Win-win."

Gus decided to ignore the pointed look from his Alpha as Zak came out of the back with two giant shopping bags full of food. What was between him and Laura was private. For now. If the time came when they decided to take things further and go public, well... He'd deal with John—and anyone else who dared raise an eyebrow at him—when the time came. For now, Gus was going to enjoy being with the woman who was fast coming to mean perhaps a bit too much to him, but he couldn't help it. She was just...perfect.

Beautiful. Desirable. Strong and damaged but working her way through her recovery. He wanted to be there for her. He wanted to be the one she reached out to in the middle of the night, or any time during the day. If the other guys dared make a stink, he'd have something to say about it. He might give the impression of being an easy-going bear, but threaten Laura, and his claws would come out.

Gus left the restaurant before he said anything else, merely nodding politely to John as he talked with Zak about something or other. Gus had places to be and a woman to seduce...if she'd let him. Boy, how he hoped she'd let him.

CHAPTER 10

Gus found Laura upstairs in her apartment when he got back to the building. She had changed out of her painting clothes, and her hair was damp, so she must have showered while he was fetching dinner. He knew she didn't have a lot of clothing. In fact, he'd been pleased to hear from one of the mer shopkeepers that Laura had spent part of the money he'd given her on a few bits of clothing. T-shirts and leggings, mostly. Inexpensive and versatile.

He knew she needed more clothes, but he had to be careful. She was a proud woman, and he didn't want to insult her by offering what she might see as "charity".

She was wearing a Grizzly Cove T-shirt in a pretty pink color. They'd allowed a few different designs to be printed, mostly to sell to tourists. John had been surprised when most of the guys and almost all the mer wanted their own Grizzly Cove T-shirt, bringing a small percentage of the profits to the town's coffers.

As the town grew, the town council, of which Gus was a part, had decided to collect small amounts from various enterprises to use for the general upkeep and as an emergency fund should anyone in town need help. They'd decided that anything bearing the town logos would pay a small percentage into the town fund. Ironically, that fund had grown faster than any of them had expected when the first order of shirts sold out in less than a week.

The initial order had been meant to supply the expected tourists that would soon come into town, once the warmer weather hit. Instead, the entire order had went to people who already lived there, and they'd had to reorder and double the quantity. A small selection of shot glasses, beer and wine glasses had also been ordered with the various approved town logos, as well as things like tote bags and beach towels. The shops were fully stocked now, in anticipation of receiving tourists.

Nobody knew exactly when or how the tourists would find the place, but everyone knew there was no way to keep curious humans out of town. Instead of shunning them, the decision had been made early on to try to welcome them as best they could, entertain them while they were here, then send them on their way, happy they had taken the detour to see the town, and perhaps spend a little money on the art produced there.

And art was something Laura was proving exceedingly proficient in making. As she escorted him into the apartment, Gus noted the little side table by the couch had that box with the antler pieces and tools in it. It looked like she'd been working at turning the raw antlers into miniature works of art.

"I hope some of those are meant to sell in the gallery," he said, nodding toward the box as he walked past on his way to the kitchen island. He set the bags down, and she took one, helping him unpack the contents as if they worked together all the time. He liked the feeling, and his inner bear approved.

"First, I wanted to make gifts for the people who've helped me," she told him as they worked side by side, "but I've got a few that I could put on display downstairs, just to fill that corner. I have enough material left to make the gifts, regardless. I just need a little time to finish them."

Gus noted a small easel set by the window, along with a stack of small, blank canvases. "Are you painting, too?"

She shrugged. "Again, some are gifts, but I'll have a couple ready for the gallery opening. I don't want that corner to be empty."

Gus wanted to tell her to forget about making gifts and concentrate on saleable goods, but he knew that wasn't going to go over well. Heck, it wouldn't have worked on him, either. There was such a thing as pride and honor. Laura seemed to have that in spades. She honored her debts, even if they had been forgiven. Pride would not let her take something for nothing, even if what she could give in return was just something small, though heartfelt. He understood, so he let it go.

"It'll all work out," he replied gently, unpacking the last of the containers while Laura turned to the cabinets to get a couple of plates and some silverware.

They shared a companionable dinner and talked about the preparations everyone in town was making to welcome tourists. They'd had a few from time to time last year, but they all expected more of an influx of human visitors this year, as soon as the weather got a little more cooperative. Though the climate of the area was reasonably temperate, there were lots of storms that made the small mountain roads that were the only way to get to Grizzly Cove somewhat treacherous for part of the year. As soon as the weather turned, people would start traveling those roads again, and as long as they weren't evil-hearted, any humans should pass right through the protective ward surrounding the town, not even realizing it was there.

If they were of evil intent, the ward would repulse them gently. It would give them the urge to turn around and go somewhere else if they were non-magical folk, who didn't even know such things as wards existed. If they were magical folk, the reaction of the ward would be stronger, and they'd be repulsed with prejudice if they tried to bully their way in magically. Urse had set up her ward with different response levels—another mark of a master mage with a once-in-several-generations gift for ward-casting.

After dinner, they lingered over coffee. Laura picked up

one of her carving pieces, shaping it absently while they talked about plans for the gallery and the gifts she was making, or planned to make, for various people who had done her a good turn while in town. Gus just liked sitting with her, talking quietly. He liked being in her presence. There was something so calming about being with her and he found her absent-minded carving as soothing as she apparently did.

When she started to yawn, he took the empty coffee cups away and rinsed them in the sink before putting them in the dishwasher. Then, he returned to the living room area and scooped her up in his arms, much to her surprise and delight. She laughed and threw her arms around his neck, just as he'd hoped, while he carried her down the hall to her bedroom.

He kissed like a dream, and now that they'd already been intimate, Laura's body knew the intensity of the pleasure he could give her. She had yearned for more of that ecstasy, and she was about to get what she'd been wanting. Gus undressed her with strong movements, ridding himself of his own clothing in record time. They were naked, together, standing at the side of the big bed, and urgency seemed to be riding them both.

Wanting something different and a little daring, Laura tugged Gus down onto the bed but turned over to look at him over her shoulder in silent invitation. She was a wolf, at heart, and sometimes, she needed to do things the wolf way. This was one of those times… If her giant teddy bear would cooperate.

Gus's sexy smile said it all. He followed her downward onto the bed. They were both breathing hard with anticipation and need. This would be hard and fast, but that's what she wanted. They were both feeling it. She could tell by the way he positioned her body under him that he was as excited by the prospect of joining with her again, as she was.

And before too much longer, he slid into her from behind. Her ass raised in the air, they did it wolf-style, the dominant male taking his female in an act as old as time, as filled with care and passion as it was urgency and need.

He stroked into her slow, at first, then speeding up as they found their rhythm. There was something so primal about the way this felt. It satisfied the wolf part of her psyche, which usually watched quietly inside while the human side was in control. But this was something the wolf understood. Something the wolf craved. Possession by its chosen partner. An act of life affirmation. An act of nature.

Scratch that. The way Gus did it, it was a *force* of nature. The pleasure built and built. The intensity of his possession made her feel...cherished, in an odd way. He was forceful, but also gentle. Strong, yet also compassionate. Fierce, tempered with care.

He was all the things she'd been yearning for and thought she would never find.

The pressure built as his motion increased. She felt the grip of his hands on her ass, her hips, moving, positioning her to his will. She felt the growl of her wolf spirit deep in her chest, and when she came, the wolf howled from inside her.

The roar of Gus's bear joined the howl of her inner wolf as he came with her in an earth-shattering climax that went on and on...and on...

When Laura came back to herself, she was lying on her side with Gus behind her in the big bed. His arm was draped loosely over her waist, and she was using one of his arms as a rather muscular pillow. He was semi-hard and still inside her.

Oh, yeah.

She felt just languid enough that she wanted to bask a little, but other things were stirring inside her. The passion that remained like a banked flame in her midsection wanted to rekindle and burst into full flame. She knew already that Gus could easily wring that sort of response from her...all night long.

She placed her hand over his on her midriff. "Thank you," she whispered, knowing he would hear her.

Gus placed a soft kiss just behind her ear that made her

shiver. "If it's in my power, I will give you anything you want, Laura. That's the simple truth," he told her in a gruff voice.

She heard the ring of certainty in his voice. He meant every word, and it touched her deeply. A little ember escaped from her tight control and rekindled the flame of passion in her body. She squeezed him where they were still joined and felt satisfaction at the evidence of renewed interest in that direction.

"Take me to the stars, again, Gus," she asked, still whispering as the invisible fire of attraction unfurled between them once more.

Gus started to move slowly. The urgency had been dulled a little, so this time, he was able to take more time with his lover. She was so special to him. More special than she knew.

Gus enjoyed everything about being with Laura. She was strong and fearless when it came to lovemaking. She knew what she wanted, and she wasn't afraid to give him direction. She was also willing to follow his lead, as she'd proven many times already. She was his perfect match in bed. Out of it? Well, he had his suspicions and beliefs, but he suspected there would be time to figure that out later. Much later.

Gus adjusted her legs so that he could penetrate more deeply. It was a slightly odd position, but the sensations were worth it. She took him deep and squeezed him until he thought he might come just from that, but he powered on, wanting to bring her to ecstasy before he found his own.

His efforts were rewarded a few minutes later when she cried out. His name. She had cried out his name in passion. That triggered his own release, and he joined her…among the stars, as she had requested.

CHAPTER 11

The next morning, when Laura woke, it was to the scent of bacon being cooked in her apartment. She smiled as she heard the soft sounds that meant Gus was up and cooking breakfast for her. Never had she had a man cook breakfast for her while she lazed in bed. She smiled as she thought about it. The men of Grizzly Cove were something else. Or maybe that was just Gus. Never had she met a kinder, sexier man than Gustav van Wilde.

He probably had some romantic notion of serving her breakfast in bed, but Laura had to get up. She went into the bathroom, took care of things and freshened up, then went out into the kitchen area to join Gus. As she'd suspected, he was loading a tray that must've been in one of the closets, but when he saw her, he adjusted easily, rerouting the large plate laden with fluffy eggs, crispy bacon and other items to the kitchen island instead.

Then, he came over to her and wrapped one strong arm around her waist, tugging her in close. Sexy move by an even sexier man. Her heart did a little flutter as her body remembered the passion he'd shown her the night before.

"Good morning," he rumbled near her ear before sliding his lips over her cheek to zero in on her lips.

Their kiss was slow, lazy, but filled with heat. She almost

told him to skip breakfast and take her back to bed, but he ended the kiss before things could go too far. He set her away from him and turned back to the stove, where he had left things cooking. She shook her head. She was glad one of them was able to focus.

Laura looked around, noticing the fresh bread on the counter near the toaster. Had he already gone out to the bakery and come back? It sure looked like it. She went over and put some slices in the toaster, wanting to help him.

"Looks like you were up early," she commented as she worked. She liked working alongside Gus. He was easy to be around, in so many ways.

"Yeah, I went across the street and picked up a few things," he said offhandedly. Laura knew the bakery was open even before dawn because Ashley got up during what Laura thought of as the middle of the night, to start work on her artisanal breads each day. "Nell was working with Ash this morning because John was doing some late-night conferencing with Master Hiram. When I got up and happened to look out the window, I saw the lights in the front of the bake shop go on. Usually, Ash keeps only the work area lights on while she's prepping her breads, and Tom is always with her. When I saw Nell in the front of the shop, I decided to go over and see what was going on. Tom was in back with Ash, so I just picked up some fresh bread and supplies and came back."

That was Gus. Checking to see if everything was okay. He seemed to look at the whole town as his responsibility. Then again, most of the bears seemed to feel that way about this town. It was amazing, really. They were all so Alpha—each in their own ways—but they all seemed to band together behind the idea of making this town and keeping everyone in it safe. The guys of Grizzly Cove were something special, all right.

When the toast popped, she brought it over to the kitchen island. There were two stools there they could sit on while eating. It was informal and perfect for the cozy morning they were sharing.

"Master Hiram," Laura said, after Gus had turned things off and taken his seat beside her with his own heaping plate of eggs, "he's the Master vampire of Seattle, right?"

Gus nodded as they both ate. "John is on good terms with Master Hiram, but of course, their communications have to be made at night, while Hiram is fully awake. John can leave messages for him during the day, but if they want a live conversation, John has to accommodate Hiram's schedule. From what I understand, Hiram has a personal secretary who keeps track of everything. Hiram's got business interests all over the world, and his working day is while this side of the world is sleeping, so he's booked pretty solid with conference calls to humans on the other side of the planet, and meetings with Others who understand Hiram's limitations. It's hard to get an appointment with him, actually, but he manages to fit John or Zak in whenever they need to talk, which we all find gratifying."

"Why's that?" she asked, just for something to say.

The very idea of being on such close terms with a bloodletter was both fascinating and a bit troublesome to her. Her Pack had been very leery of the bloodletters that went north to take advantage of the long winter nights. Of course, most of those stuck to the cities where there was more and easier prey for their kind, but the occasional vampire passed through, making everyone more vigilant. Shifter blood was more powerful to their kind than human blood, and they would seek it if they thought they could get away with it.

The entire Pack went on alert whenever a bloodletter was known to be in the area, and the weakest of the Pack were protected at all times of darkness by the strongest of the Pack. That's just the way it worked in a healthy Pack. It reminded her of the way the bears of Grizzly Cove looked out for each other and everyone under their protection. She'd missed Pack life, but Grizzly Cove was similar, if not even a little bit better for someone like her.

She thought privately that she might feel a bit smothered in a Pack setting after her ordeal. They would mean well, of course, but wolf Packs were all about togetherness, and right now, Laura felt like she needed a bit of alone time to settle back into her human skin. Grizzly Cove was giving her the space she needed, but also the camaraderie and protective feeling a wolf Pack gave its members. It was the perfect place, really, for her to recover.

"Well, Master Hiram put a portion of his money into Zak's restaurant. He's the silent partner, in fact. And, when he washed ashore after the leviathan chomped on his yacht, killing his entire crew and injuring him almost beyond repair—even for a vampire—he proved to be a man of his word. The relationship between him and Zak was cemented that night, and his understanding with John wasn't far behind."

"Why Zak? I thought John was the Alpha and Brody his second. Where does Zak fit in?" she asked as they ate.

"Zak was the first one to encounter Hiram, and he allowed Hiram to drink his blood in order to protect Tina, who was also part of that initial confrontation. A bond formed between them because of that link. I've asked Zak about it, but he won't say much. I think the bloodletter is more aware of the bond than the victim—or, in this case, donor. But it's definitely there. Zak is linked to Hiram now. A small magical tendril stretches between them."

"That's really interesting," Laura said, meaning every word. She had little to no experience with bloodletters. Even the *Venifucus* who had held her captive didn't deal with the ancient immortals all that often.

Gus went on to describe that initial meeting with the Master of Seattle in more detail as they ate, but eventually, his tale wound down, and the food was gone. Any excuse to linger and not begin their day was rapidly diminishing as the sun rose higher in the sky. Reluctantly, it seemed, they both got up and tidied up the kitchen, pausing here and there to share a smooch or loving touch. It was fun, working with Gus, even at such a mundane chore as cleaning the kitchen.

They kept up the banter and lighthearted flirting as they

moved down to the gallery and set to work. They worked together all morning, setting up displays on the side of the room that was ready. The tribe's wares were a pleasure to handle and exhibit, and the tone and feel of the art pieces worked well with the subtle shades of the murals on the walls. Everything complemented everything else, which gave Laura a deep sense of satisfaction.

She'd been afraid, when she saw the luxurious colors and textures of the art and jewelry items the tribe had given into Gus's care, that her murals would clash, somehow. But it had all worked out. The murals merely set the scene, allowing the pieces to shine in their own right.

Gus had been working on subtle changes to the miniature track lighting that was concealed in the ceiling. Laura hadn't known about it until he'd turned it on and started focusing the small lights on various items in the display, setting them off beautifully. He really had an eye for that sort of thing, and she was surprised to learn that she loved setting up the sales area and, of course, working alongside Gus.

Laura was alone in the gallery for a few minutes while Gus went to get lunch. She was putting the finishing touches on another section of the cabinet along the long wall when she heard the door to the gallery open. Expecting Gus, she smiled as she turned, only to be surprised by someone completely different.

One of the old ladies she had seen at the stone circle stood near the doorway, taking her time looking around as if she owned the place. Laura's smile faltered a bit, but she wanted to be friendly.

"Hello." Laura greeted the woman, unsure of her footing. The old lady wasn't looking at Laura, but at the displays. She was looking at them as if evaluating them. Laura stepped forward hesitantly. She had no idea what to do in this situation. Elders were revered in her culture. She would try to be patient, but she was in a new country, among new people, where traditions were different, which made her unsure about what the proper response should be.

Just when Laura was about to try speaking with the woman again, the old lady turned her deep brown, penetrating gaze on Laura. "It is good to see you looking healthier than when you arrived here," the lady began, her voice heavily accented. She sounded sort of...Russian, maybe? Laura wasn't that great with accents. "Everyone here calls me *Babushka*. Is Russian for grandma, yes?" She didn't wait for Laura to answer. "Really, I am grandma to Peter only, but I like his friends and treat them like I would treat my own grand-cubs."

Laura had a little trouble following the old lady's words—mostly because of the accent—but she thought she got the gist of it. She seemed friendly, in a foreign sort of way.

"Do you know Kamchatka?" Laura only had time to shake her head in the negative before Babushka went on. "Is Siberia. Very wild. Coastal. I have many relatives there with little enough opportunity to make money. I have talked to Gustav about this, and he mentioned possibility of Kamchatka art displayed here." She turned to survey the room once more. "I like what you have done," she pronounced, and Laura felt unaccountably flattered, though she really didn't know this rather eccentric woman. "Paint this wall for Kamchatka, and we will do brisk business. I will provide inspirational photos. Tell Gustav. I return tomorrow to discuss display." With that, she headed for the door, pausing with her hand on the knob to look back at Laura and smile. "I am glad you are recovered. Be well, little wolf." The kind words sounded like a benediction, and Laura felt emotion well in her heart as the old lady left the room.

Only after Babushka was gone did Laura realize she'd only gotten one word out. The Russian grandma was a force to be reckoned with. No doubt about it.

Gus came in a few minutes later while Laura was still marveling at the exchange. "Was that Peter's grandmother I saw coming out of the building? Did she stop in here?" he asked.

Laura couldn't help the giggle that bubbled up from

somewhere. The old lady's behavior was amusing in retrospect. She was scary, but the encounter had been harmless enough. Laura told Gus all about it as they moved upstairs to eat lunch.

"Sounds like she likes you," Gus observed, when Laura told him about Babushka's parting words. "You could do a lot worse than have that woman on your side. She is one scary bear, even as old as she is. Have you ever heard about Kamchatka bears?"

"No. I've never even heard of the place before. She said it was part of Siberia?"

"It's a peninsula off the coast. Very rugged. Very isolated," Gus told her. "The bears there are huge and very fierce, though they don't interact with humans much. There was one occasion, though, a few years back, when a mining company did something the local Clan didn't like, and there was not only bloodshed, but the bears surrounded the compound where the miners were living and blockaded the place. They wouldn't let the men out for a week. Made the international news and everything. Humans thought it was pretty strange, but after the hubbub died down, the Clan got concessions from the mining company."

"You mean the mining company knew to negotiate with the Clan? I thought shifters weren't supposed to reveal themselves." Laura was confused.

"They didn't. The Clan is a large part of the local government, and the miners didn't realize the crazy bears were also the tough politicians they had been negotiating with. Though, it was a close thing. Those bears are a little nuts. They take big risks. Peter's just the same, but I've never met a man with a truer heart. He's a good guy, even if he does have a slightly insane berserker side." Gus chuckled at his own words. "That family has dragon blood, or so they claim."

"Dragon? Like fire-breathing giant lizard, *dragon*?" Laura was astounded.

Gus nodded. "Shifter dragon."

"There really is such a thing? I thought dragons were a myth."

"They're incredibly rare, and they were hunted after the last time the world fought the Destroyer. Some went into hiding. Others—many others—were killed. Babushka's line descends from a dragon shifter who mated with one of her ancestors. She knew him when she was little."

"That's amazing," Laura said. "And kind of sad. I hate to think of any shifter being hunted like that."

They finished their meal and lingered over coffee to discuss the gallery.

"There's really only enough unique pieces from the local tribe to cover the displays we just set up. The remainder of the stock will stay in the store room and be used to replenish, since a lot of it is duplicates of the same, or similar, items," Gus noted. "That leaves plenty of room for Kamchatka arts and crafts on that other wall."

"What kinds of things do you think they'll send?" Laura asked as she sipped her coffee.

"I know Peter's granny makes nesting dolls, only they're not people. They're bears." Gus smiled at her over the rim of his coffee mug.

"Nesting bears?" Laura mused, chuckling. "Sounds funny to me. Birds nest."

Gus laughed and shook his head. "They're cute. You'll see," he told her. "I'm not sure what the rest of the Clan does, but it'll lend an exotic feel to the gallery, I bet. Nobody else in town had Russian stuff. Babushka set up a little stall for a while next to Peter's shop, but I think she got bored with running it, especially since we haven't had many tourists yet. She uses the space mainly as a workshop." He sipped his coffee then broached a new subject. "How about the corner where the white wolf is painted? I hope you're planning to put some of your own work there. Do you have enough supplies? I can get you canvases if you want to paint, or more antlers if you want to carve."

She was pleased by his offer, and his thoughtfulness. "I've

got enough antler for now," she told him. "As soon as I finish making the gifts I'm giving to the people who have helped me, I'll start work on items for sale. Do you really think folks will want to buy them?"

"Honey, if your murals are anything to go by, you're going to be famous for your art. Mark my words," he told her, beaming his approval.

"I don't really want to be famous," she replied, truthfully. "I'd rather just be able to make enough money to pay my bills and have a bit of financial security."

"I wouldn't worry about that," he said, his expression full of confidence in her abilities. "You're going to do very well, indeed."

"Is that a Shamanistic proclamation?" she teased.

Gus tilted his head. "Something like that," he replied, surprising her. "I just know you're going to do well. Your art has spirit. It speaks to the soul. People will see that and want to have it in their homes. Guaranteed. So, you'd better get cracking on something to display. When people see these murals, they're going to want smaller versions to take home." He thought for a moment, then seemed to get an idea. "In fact, we could have photographs taken of the murals and made into postcards or note cards they could buy in the shop. What do you think? I could have them printed up, and you, as the artist, would get any profit above the cost of printing."

"That doesn't seem fair," she said, right away. "The gallery should get some of the profit, since I made the murals for the gallery."

Gus scowled. "Ten percent towards overhead for the gallery, which I consider very generous of you. Not a penny more. You're the artist. They're buying your art."

"Well, all right. If you're sure. I just hope people want to buy them, because if not, we'll be out the cost of printing with nothing to show for it." Worry made her bite her lower lip.

Gus slid forward on his chair and kissed her, using his tongue to soothe the spot on her lip she'd worried. When he drew back, his gaze met hers. His smile was gentle.

"Trust me, sweetheart. This is going to work better than you can even imagine." He sat back, and a mischievous light entered his eyes. "I will even offer the cards up for sale on the gallery's website. I think people all over the world will be buying them without even having to see the murals in person. Wait and see."

"The internet?" she asked, still unsure about the technological terms for things she had yet to encounter.

Gus nodded, grinning. "I'll show it to you, and I bet you'll want to know more. In a little while, you'll be online shopping with the best of 'em. Guaranteed."

CHAPTER 12

Later that afternoon, Babushka arrived armed with photos of her homeland. Gus left the ladies to their discussions after greeting Babushka with a warm hug. The old lady watched him go with a speculative gaze that settled on Laura.

"He is good man, that one. Powerful, but his strength is tempered with a pure spirit," Babushka offered her opinion seemingly out of thin air.

Laura nodded. "I have met shaman before. I don't underestimate his gentle appearance. I know he is fierce."

"And gentle," Babushka reminded her. "He is different than other bears. He walks a more spiritual path." The older woman's eyes narrowed. "Where did you know shaman?"

"Among the Inuit," Laura told her.

"Human holy men?" Babushka wasn't exactly dismissive, but she didn't seem all that impressed, either. "It is a sacred thing for a shifter who can see the Goddess in action. Your Gustav is more special than you probably realize."

That said, Babushka brandished a large envelope that seemed stuffed with paper. She put it down on the counter to the side of where the register had just been installed and opened it.

"Photos of my homeland," she said without preamble. "Coastline. Forests. Local wildlife." She spread the photos

113

out across the wide counter as Laura bent closer to get a good look. "Is similar to Pacific Northwest in places. Probably more like Alaska coast because of climate. See?" She pointed to the rocky shore and the lush dark green of the forest.

Laura was getting great ideas for her mural. She could already see it taking shape in her mind's eye. All she needed to know was more about the kinds of bears in that rugged land.

"I've heard your bear is much larger than others," Laura said quietly, trying not to be rude. "And that your fur is more burgundy than brown."

"This is true. We are mostly big. Like Kodiak bears. Have you seen?" Laura shook her head in the negative. Babushka shrugged. "No matter. Take grizzly shifter and add ten percent. And fur is different. Denser. More red. Not like Soviet flag, but like fine dark wine," she said, chuckling. "Though, of course, we prefer strong vodka to fruity wine."

She laughed some more as Laura studied the photos. She had a strong idea of what she would paint. It wasn't complete yet, but she'd get there.

"Now," Babushka went on, reaching for the large satchel she'd been carrying but had put on the ground as they talked. She lifted it and reached in with one hand. "Gifts. This, for Gustav. Is, like Sheriff Brody carves with his chainsaw, a self-portrait...of me." She placed a carved box in the shape of a bear on the counter, a big smile on her lined face. The bear had burgundy fur.

"Is it a nesting box?" Laura asked in wonder. The workmanship was exquisite.

Babushka smiled gently at her. "Try and see."

With great care, Laura took the box into her hands and opened it. Sure enough, there was another smaller box inside. It was just as beautiful, with just as much attention to detail. She opened that one, and there was another inside. And another. And another. All together, there were five burgundy Kamchatka bear boxes, and each one was gorgeous.

"Oh, Gus is going to love this," Laura enthused. "It's

fantastic."

Before she could say anything else, Babushka reached into her bag again, and came out with another box carved in the shape of a bear—this one with the unmistakable creamy coat of the spirit bear. Laura's breath caught in admiration.

"This is for you, Laura. A welcome gift." Babushka handed the box to Laura, who took it with stunned appreciation.

"It's Gus, isn't it?" Laura asked, breathless as she looked from the box to the old woman and back again.

"It is. Just like you have painted him," Babushka added, looking pointedly at the mural of the giant sequoia and the cream-colored bear. "He is a special one, that boy."

Only a bear as old as Babushka would ever be able to call Gus a *boy*, Laura thought with some amusement. But the old lady was right. Gus was special. Laura's little heart went pitter-pat just thinking about him. She had better change the subject before she gave herself away.

"Thank you so much for the gift," she said, already planning a gift she would make for Babushka in return. "Is it true... I mean... I don't want to be rude, but Gus said something about there being a... um... dragon in town. He seemed to imply he was a relation of yours."

Babushka looked at Laura with an appraising eye for a long moment before she spoke. "It is not something we used to discuss, but everything about this town is not normal." She chuckled at her own small joke. "My grandfather was dragon. The dragon who came here recently is distant relation, but we claim him as family. Poor boy grew up as an orphan among humans." Babushka shook her head, clicking her tongue with a disapproving sound. "He is good man, but is hard for a dragon alone in the world. He is part of our Clan now. I have adopted him, as the Americans say." She smiled at that, and her expression lightened. "So, cat—or *dragon*, in this case—is definitely out of bag now, I suppose." She shrugged philosophically.

Babushka left the gallery a short time later, and Laura set right to work on the mural of Kamchatka. She already knew what she was going to paint and that she was going to put a tiny figure flying in the distance that might look like a smudge to most casual observers, but any shifter in town would know what it really was. A dragon. A *shifter* dragon. Just the idea of there being such a creature in this world boggled Laura's mind.

She painted, thinking about how cool it would be to actually see a real dragon flying overhead. Who knew? Maybe, if she stayed in Grizzly Cove long enough, that daydream might just happen.

She filled in the trees and foliage working from the photographs Babushka had left behind, leaving space for several large bears walking along the shoreline. She wanted to depict a family containing several generations from cubs to venerable old Babushka. The vignette formed in her mind and transferred rapidly onto the wall as her brush stroked paint over the flat surface in strategic ways.

Lost in the work, she almost didn't notice when the outer door to the building opened, but when the door to the gallery clicked open a moment later, she got a distinctly uncomfortable feeling between her shoulder blades and a flash of pain behind her eyes. She turned, gasping, as she came face to face with the newcomer.

It was the Alpha bear. John Marshall. Arguably, the most powerful of the bears gathered here, because he led them all. She knew this. She's met him before. But this time… This time, something was different.

That inner…*thing*…that had been stretching and growing and growling inside her was looking at him through her eyes, and the hatred it felt stunned her. She froze. Her muscles went into a sort of rigor as the paintbrush fell from her hand. She stared at him, a helpless observer in her own body as something *evil* pushed to get out. To get at *him*.

"You have to leave," she sobbed, even as she tried to hold back the power that was building. "Please!" She still couldn't move. "Go! Before it hurts you!"

John's steps faltered as he looked more closely at her. Whatever he saw must have convinced him of…something. He turned on his heel and shouted over his shoulder as he exited. "I'm getting help!"

The moment he was out of sight, she sagged, still not quite in control of her body, but definitely closer to it than just seconds before. It was as if the Alpha bear had taken the compulsion with him when he left her presence. She had a dreadful fear that she knew what that meant.

He was a trigger. Seeing him would spark an attack from whatever it was those evil bastards had planted inside her. She hoped he was smart enough to realize what he'd been seeing and not to come back into her line of sight.

She stood there, not daring to move even as she regained control of her body. She felt really strange. As if something had broken loose inside her. Like some alien awareness that thirsted for violence was just waiting to use her for its own evil ends.

Tears started to fall unheeded down her face. She should have known it was all too good to be true. She had been starting to believe that she might just be able to have a fresh start here in Grizzly Cove, but now, that dream was crashing down around her feet.

They wouldn't let her stay. Not when it was clear that something had been done to her while she'd been held prisoner for so long. Something had *changed*. She didn't feel right. She knew, on a fundamental level, that somehow, someone had done something to use her against her will.

She was a sleeper agent. A Trojan Horse. An unwilling accomplice to plans others had made to attack Grizzly Cove—and, in particular, the Alpha bear who had brought this town together. It came so clear to her suddenly. They had well and truly fucked her over. Not only had she been prisoner for so very long that she had retreated to another realm to get at least partial escape, but they'd hedged their bets. Her captors had turned her into an unwilling weapon, as surely as a child put in a bomb vest by some insane fanatic, to do their bidding.

She was so screwed.

She was going to lose everything she had thought she had just regained. Marilee. Gus. The town she was coming to love. The people she had befriended here. It was all going up in a puff of smoke before her streaming eyes.

She sank to her knees in utter despair, sobbing for all she was worth.

Gus approached the building at a run. John was standing just outside the building, in the street, watching the entrance carefully, out of view of the windows. He'd called Gus and filled him in. Luckily, Gus hadn't been too far away. He'd been just down the street, working on something with another of the guys when the call came in.

He'd dropped everything and hit the ground running as soon as he heard what John said. Something was wrong with Laura, and John had retreated at her demand. It looked like what they'd feared might actually be true. She might have been programmed by her captors to lash out at John or the other residents of Grizzly Cove, and the programming was only just coming into play.

Gus swore as he slowed to confer with John. He would go in—he was the only one who could—but he wanted to know everything that had been observed, first. John didn't wait. He started his sitrep the moment Gus was in range and talked fast and concise, as they'd all been trained to do, providing facts, observations and, in John's case, suggestions and encouragement. He wasn't their leader for nothing.

As fully prepared as possible, Gus walked into the building and then approached the door to the gallery, which was still wide open. He saw her at once, kneeling on the ground, crying her heart out.

Pain sliced through his being. She looked absolutely heartbroken, and he thought he understood why. The Laura he had come to know—had come to love—was a good person. She would never have looked crosswise at John or anyone else. That something had made her go rigid and warn him off meant that something was very wrong, and Gus was very much afraid he knew, at least generally, what it was.

"Laura, love... Are you all right, now?" Gus spoke softly, approaching her cautiously.

At his words, she looked up, tears making wide tracks down her cheeks. Her face was scrunched up in pain and regret, but at least she didn't look like she was about to let loose with a magic lightning bolt and fry his ass or anything. He moved closer, crouching down in front of her.

"It almost took over," she whispered, hiccupping with the sobs that still tore through her shaking body. "It almost lashed out at John."

"Is it still there, trying to take over?" he asked cautiously. "Or are you in control, now?"

She tilted her head, seeming to consider his words as her tears slowed. "I think it's gone. It wanted John. It *hated* John."

"But it doesn't hate me?" he asked with a small grin, trying to coax her out of her crying completely.

"It doesn't have any say in the matter. *I* don't hate you. Not by a long shot." She reached out for him then, and he took her into his arms, hating the way she trembled in fear and sadness.

He stood, lifting her in his arms as he walked out of the gallery and toward the back stairs that would lead up to the apartments. He knew John would see them. Gus had no doubt that more than just John was now watching everything that went on in the building, from the shadows. As long as Laura didn't see them, Gus figured whatever was hurting her from the inside out wouldn't activate. Whatever she felt for him seemed to countermand any desire the internal programming might have where he was concerned...at least, for now.

He would take advantage of that for as long as he could. He wanted to stop whatever it was and free her of the evil taint. He wasn't letting her go—not to death, nor to exile.

BIANCA D'ARC

They had to find another way. He would not release her that easily. She was in his heart now, and he would keep her there, always.

Marilee was at the top of the stairs to greet them. John must have called ahead, knowing that if Laura hadn't hurt Gus, then she definitely wouldn't harm her only child. Marilee looked frightened but determined to help. Still, Gus wasn't going to expose her to an unknown level of danger, right now. It was enough that he took the chance of whatever was inside Laura blowing up in his face. He wouldn't allow Marilee to take that same chance. Not to the same extent, at least. He wouldn't deny the mother and daughter a few moments to talk, but he wasn't going to expose either of them too long, just in case.

Still, it was handy she was there, because right about now, he could use a little help getting the door to Laura's apartment open. He gestured with a jerk of his chin, and Marilee took the hint. She even had her own key.

"Mama gave me the key only yesterday," Marilee said to Gus as she unlocked the door. Laura had hidden her face in Gus's neck, apparently not ready to face her child, just yet.

Gus walked past the younger woman and into the apartment once she had the door open. "I'll take care of her," he promised Marilee. She looked so worried and so sad, his heart went out to this younger version of Laura. "She is strong. She'll be okay."

He could feel Laura shaking in his arms, but she lifted her head to look at her daughter as Gus placed her on the couch. Her eyes were streaming with tears again. Damn. He'd thought that had stopped.

"I'm so sorry, honey," Laura said, looking straight at her daughter. "I thought I was okay, but I'm not. It's clear, now, that they...did something to me. I'm going to have to leave."

"No!" Marilee said forcefully, even as Gus shook his head.

"Honey, if you think I'm letting you leave here under these conditions, you don't know me at all." Laura turned her attention to him, confusion on her lovely face. "We'll fix this.

120

I know we can."

Laura's eyes narrowed. The crying had stopped again, thank goodness, but now, she regarded him with a bit of suspicion.

"You were watching for this, weren't you?" She looked so...betrayed. Angry and pale, as if the thought that he hadn't quite trusted everything about her was so foreign as to be abhorrent.

Gus sighed. "I've been honest with you from the beginning, if not completely open. I will admit, now that I am free to do so, that Big John asked me to keep an eye on you for just this kind of thing. He was concerned that the mages who had control over you for so many years might have done something to you. Something that you didn't know consciously about. So, I've been keeping my eyes open. That's all." He wiped a frustrated hand through his hair. "I agreed to it because I wanted to look out for you. I wanted to protect you."

As admissions went, his wasn't very eloquent, and it wasn't particularly well received. Drat. She was going to be hurt and angry, just as he'd feared, but at this point, it couldn't be helped. He had been committed to this path from the moment John had guilted him into agreement with his request. Dammit.

"You were going to attack John, right? Am I right in thinking you were feeling some kind of compulsion?" Gus asked gently. She nodded mutely. Gus shook his head once, looking weary. "John thought so. That's what he told me it looked like on the phone. He also said it looked like you were fighting it."

"I was immobilized by it," she admitted, blowing out a frustrated breath. Now that she was coming down from the terror-filled high, she was getting angry. Scared, still, but angry, too.

"But you told him to leave. You warned him as best you could," Gus insisted. "That's what he told me."

Laura just shook her head. How could she explain it when she didn't understand it all herself?

Marilee reached out to touch her hand. Laura almost flinched away from the sudden contact, but it was her *daughter*. She would never hurt her baby by such an action. She couldn't. Not if every demon in hell tried to force her to do so.

There was that, at least. Marilee…and Gus, too…seemed to be safe from the danger she posed. But was Marilee's mate? Laura didn't dare take the chance to find out. And the thing that bothered her most… Was the compulsion going to grow even stronger? It seemed to have taken time to get to this point. Would it get even bigger? Would it consume her?

She didn't know the answers to any of it. Tears gathered behind her eyes again. She had just regained her life, and now, was she to lose it all over again? This time, forever?

"Go back to King, Lee Lee," Laura told her daughter. "I need a little time on my own to think this through." Laura turned her hand over to grasp her daughter's. Would this be the last time she ever saw her baby? So much was uncertain. "I love you, sweetheart. Never forget that."

"I love you too, Mama," Laura replied, a catch in her voice. She bent down to give her mother a hug and kiss on the cheek. She straightened and left the apartment, but not without exchanging a significant look with Gus.

Laura looked at Gus as Marilee left. Her lover. Or her keeper?

CHAPTER 13

"I'm going to have to leave," Laura repeated herself, but Gus was shaking his head.

"No, honey. Not by a long shot," he told her, taking the seat beside her on the couch. Crowding her. Not letting her run away, either physically or mentally, from the harsh reality that had just revealed itself in full.

"You can't keep me here. I'm dangerous," she tried to reason with him.

"What if I said I liked danger?" he asked, a little smile curving one corner of his mouth. Talented mouth. A mouth that made her think of things better left alone considering their circumstances.

"Then, I'd say you're crazy," she huffed, getting up from the couch and starting to pace along the wall of windows facing the cove. The view was tremendous, but she didn't see it. All she saw was a new kind of imprisonment. "Even if I stay in Grizzly Cove, I can't go out among people. Forget about running the gallery for you. I'd be a virtual prisoner up here, all alone." She stopped walking and turned to face him. "Never again, Gus. Never."

All the terror she felt at the mere thought of being unable to come and go as she pleased, now that she had tasted freedom, filled her with dread. How could she stay in this town, knowing that every person she saw might trigger some kind of deadly magical response, over which she had, seemingly, no control.

"All right." Gus sighed, perfectly serious, once again. Thank goodness. "Let's take this down a notch. Let's go back to the beginning."

He sounded so reasonable. She had no idea what he thought he might accomplish, but she was willing to explore other options, even though she knew there were precious few courses of action open to her. She was going to have to run away. Maybe in the middle of the night when nobody was looking. She was going to have to flee, in order to protect those that she loved. Marilee…and…Gus.

Damn. She really did love him. Only now, when she had to leave him, would she allow herself to think about the inevitable truth. She loved him. More than life itself. She would do anything to protect him.

Including leave him.

Gus didn't like the look on Laura's face. She looked as if she was plotting something. Like an escape. He couldn't allow it for a whole host of reasons, not the least of which was that she was his mate. If she left, he would follow. If she ran, he would chase, even if that wasn't typically something bears were known for. He'd do just about anything for Laura, but he wouldn't let her leave in such a state. Not when there was every possibility that he, or members of the extended Grizzly Cove community, could help rid her of whatever those evil bastards had done to her.

He just had to convince her to give him a chance. Time. He needed time to marshal their resources and come up with a plan for how to help her. No way would he let her think for one more moment that anyone here wished her harm or wanted her to go now that her problem had been revealed. But how to convince her when she was already halfway gone somewhere else in her mind?

She didn't want to stand and fight. That was as clear as

day, written all over the stubborn little lift of her chin. It was up to him to find the right words to convince her to give him a chance. To give *them* a chance.

"Do you feel any violence toward me, right now?" he asked, trying to be serious and take this down to a more analytical, less emotional, level.

"Only if you try to tell me I can't leave," she replied, her words a verbal lash.

Gus held up both his hands, palms outward. "Honey, if it comes to that, I'll go with you. I won't let you face this—whatever it is—alone, okay?"

That seemed to set her back a bit. She rocked back on her heels physically, and her expression changed from anger to guardedness. He wasn't sure what that meant, exactly, but at least she was listening.

"Come on, Laura," he cajoled gently. "Let's try to figure this out. Let's take the first step of many toward resolving this problem."

"You really think it can be resolved?" She took a step closer to him. He had remained on the couch, and she came over to stand near it, though she didn't seem calm enough to sit, yet.

"I can promise you, right now, that I will do everything in my power to straighten this out. I'll call in every favor ever owed to me. I'll contact every person I think might be able to help. I'll beseech the Goddess, Herself, on your behalf," he said, rising and taking Laura's hands in both of his. "I'll do anything I can to help you."

"Why?" she whispered, unmoving, but a cautious sort of hope shining in her eyes.

"Because that's what a man does for a woman he cares about," he answered, surprising himself. He hadn't expected to make any declarations today, but fate had conspired to make him speak. When he saw the wonder dawning over her face, he knew he'd been right to follow his instincts.

"You...um...care for me?" Laura asked, still whispering, as if a harsh word would break the tender moment.

Gus nodded solemnly. "I do," he confirmed.

"Oh, Gus." She looked down and away as his heart broke. She didn't care for him at all.

Wait. She didn't? No way. She *had to*! His bear fairly roared in the confusion of his mind. Then, she looked back up at him.

"I care a lot for you, too, but it's impossible."

He placed her hands on his chest, covering them with his own. "Nothing is impossible."

"I wish I had your confidence," she told him. "I just don't see how this can work out." She shook her head. "I wanted to kill John. Not just attack and hurt, but kill. Dead."

"That wasn't you, honey," he reassured her. "It was something dark placed upon you. We're going to get it off." He tugged her in close and hugged her tight.

Gus was such a good man. He held her and comforted her. He made her promises she had no idea how he intended to keep, but he made them, nonetheless. She could hear the conviction in his voice. He really believed he could help her, but she still didn't see how.

"Now, before we get back to the important stuff," he told her with a small grin as he let her go, "let's talk about what happened with John. He's waiting—impatiently, I'm sure— for me to give him an update."

The reminder that they had been watching her all this time annoyed her a bit, but she tried to let it go. They'd been right to worry, after all. Even Laura hadn't known for sure if those evil mages had done something to her that she was unaware of. Sadly, it seemed, they had. And now, everything she had dreamed of having in her life since she had woken up was on the line.

It was already lost, in fact. Gus might think there was a way to salvage this situation, but Laura was more of a realist. So much had been taken from her already. She almost believed it was her destiny to be robbed of everything...even hope.

They had taken her daughter away from her. They'd taken

over two decades of her life. They'd taken her liberty. Her freedom. They'd even robbed her of consciousness, itself, when she'd fled halfway into the faerie realm. Now, it seemed, what she had regained in coming back to this mortal realm was to be forfeited, as well.

If she wasn't so weary of it all, she would fight. But what was the point?

Laura didn't realize she had been speaking her thoughts aloud until Gus responded.

"Are you sure there isn't some kind of compulsion on your instincts, to repress your fighting spirit? This isn't you, Laura," he told her, the slightest desperation sounding in his tone. It made her sit up and think.

"Damn. I sound like Eeyore. That isn't like me," she observed, as if from afar. Something was definitely odd here.

"You can say that again," Gus rumbled, shaking his head. "Where's that ferocious wolf spirit? This isn't you talking, honey. Fight it while you tell me exactly what you felt when you saw John, and what you're feeling now, okay?"

She tried her best to do as he asked. They talked for what felt like hours, though she had no real sense of how much time had passed. She concentrated on his questions, trying to answer them to the best of her ability. She did her best to look at the situation objectively, though she knew her objectivity wasn't the greatest. Not when her anger was sparking with each new question—and each new realization—about what had been done to her while she was powerless to resist.

After much questioning, it became apparent that Laura could fight the compulsion where Gus, and Marilee, were concerned, but definitely not John...or, perhaps, anyone else. With Marilee living across the hall, Gus devised a stop-gap solution.

"It's not ideal, and it's not permanent, but until we can come up with a solid strategy, I think you should stay up here in the apartment," Gus told her. "There's less chance of your seeing anyone else and being triggered, if you hole up here for a bit."

"How long?" she asked, hating the very idea of being a prisoner, again. Even if it was in a comparatively gilded cage.

"Long enough for me to get help. I want to consult the magic circle and see if any of them can help you," he told her.

"And if they can't?" she countered.

"Then, I'll call some other folks I know and ask for their help. I'm not without resources. There are many avenues we can try before we run out of options."

She really didn't like the sound of that, but she let it go. If worse came to worst, she would shift and run. No bear could catch a wolf at full speed. She'd run far and fast and right the hell out of Grizzly Cove.

Her enemies might find her, again. In fact, she was pretty sure they were just waiting on the other side of the ward to pick her up. She almost welcomed the confrontation. She would not be taken alive, this time, and she'd take a few of them with her. The white wolf on a rampage was not something anyone wanted to see, and few would live to tell the tale of it.

That thought firmly in mind, she let Gus make his plans. It couldn't hurt to humor him for a little while. She would try to make the best of whatever time they had left together before she got fed up with the apartment and made her break.

Gus called his Alpha and made his report while, inwardly, Laura seethed. Even the sound of John's voice on the other end of the phone was enough to send her off. Magical power gathered in her body, wanting release, but she fought it down. She could not harm Gus. Never in a million years.

The Alpha bear, on the other hand, was fair game.

Laura knew that wasn't right. She shouldn't be thinking of the kind Alpha in such violent terms. That wasn't her. It was the compulsion talking. She had to be strong and fight it. She couldn't let those bastards win. Not again.

Gus took her to bed that night, and they slept in each other's arms. They hadn't talked about the declarations they had made earlier. Everything was too raw, too ragged. They didn't make love, but she had never felt more strongly loved in all her life as Gus held her through the night, stroking her hair and her back, lending his enormous strength to reassure her as she alternately wept and slept in jagged snatches of time.

He was there for her, throughout. No matter what time it was, he held her, crooning comfort in her ear, rumbling the sounds that reassured her deep in his chest. His bear was very close to the surface. It spoke to her wild wolf spirit, calming the nervous animal inside her.

He was such a good man.

The next morning dawned gray with the threat of rain. The overcast sky matched Laura's mood. The depression hadn't left her. She was more aware that it wasn't a natural byproduct of her personality. Such a defeatist attitude went counter to everything she had been before captivity. Her personality had always been a strong one. She'd always been very sure of her path. Sometimes, to her detriment.

In fact, she wondered, not for the first time, if her stubborn refusal to listen to any other than her own thoughts had caused her to make grievous mistakes. Had the obviously mistaken certainty she had felt that Roger was her one true mate led her right into the enemy's hands? Had her stubbornness led to her own downfall?

Laura was very much afraid that it had.

Thinking about the past only added to the weight of her depression. She had the sense that it was not normal, but she still felt it very strongly. It was a burden pressing down on her spirit, her soul. It made her want to give up and just…not move.

That's when she had a Eureka moment. Perhaps this depression—this immobilizing force—was designed deliberately to keep her here, in Grizzly Cove, well in sight of the people the enemy wanted her to attack. Sweet Mother of All!

Laura got up off the couch and started to pace. The wall

of windows, thankfully, faced the cove. There was not much chance she would see any of the people that might trigger a violent response if she looked out those windows. Gus had even gone so far as to arrange for an *Off Limits* sign to be placed on both ends of the beach she could see from her windows. He wasn't blacking out her windows and taking away her only view of freedom. Instead, he was trying to restrict everyone else.

Gus had left just after dawn, leaving her to sleep a bit more. Surprisingly, she had fallen back asleep and woke sometime after nine. Of course, the pall that had come over her might be responsible. Depression often resulted in excessive sleeping, at least it did for her. She'd done a lot of sleeping in captivity before she'd discovered she could retreat most of her consciousness into the faerie realm.

She got up and took her time showering and dressing. She wasn't sure what she would do with her time today. She ate some breakfast, though she wasn't all that hungry, then decided to work on her art. Not the gifts she'd been making for people. Her heart wasn't in those today.

Instead, she picked up a blank canvas and sat by the windows, utilizing the natural light that came in through them to illuminate her work. She started slowly, painting her feelings onto the plain white fabric. Soon, she was engrossed in the work, the muted colors forming and swirling to her plan, telling a tale of sadness that reflected her mood.

The canvases she had procured were small. The largest was about eleven inches by sixteen, and going down in size from there. She'd even found a few smallish circular canvases, and other odd shapes. The relatively small size meant they didn't take long to paint. When she finished with her "sorrow" depiction, she set that aside to dry and picked up a fresh canvas.

This one, she wanted to be bolder. Splashes of color and broad strokes helped her get across her frustration and anger at being a prisoner again. She was almost finished with this "anger" portrait when Gus arrived. She looked at the clock, only then realizing the morning was long over, and she had totally skipped lunch. She still wasn't that hungry, but her interest piqued at the aromas coming from the shopping bag Gus carried in with him.

"I brought food," he told her as he paused by the kitchen island. "I wasn't sure if you'd eaten already."

"I didn't," she said, putting her brush aside and rising. She stretched, surprised by how long she'd sat in on place. Her muscles were stiff. "What did you bring?"

"Barbeque," he answered succinctly, as he started removing containers from the bag. "I asked Zak to go light on the spices for you."

They ate together while Gus told her what he'd been up to all morning that had kept him from his lunch until now. Apparently, he'd been discussing her situation with the so-called magic circle of Grizzly Cove. Urse had been particularly confident that they could do something to help, and her sister, Mellie, was thinking about different potions that might counteract some of what had been done to Laura.

They both wanted to examine Laura more closely to see if they could discern exactly what kinds of compulsions might have been laid upon her, but Gus hadn't told them yes or no, just yet. He'd wanted to talk it over with Laura first, to see what she thought. If they did allow the witch sisters access, it would have to be under very controlled circumstances because either, or both, of the women might arouse the evil magic and cause Laura to do something that she would regret.

"I'm willing to try it, but I really don't want to hurt anyone. If either one of them triggers my programming, I don't really know what will happen," Laura said, defeat and fear in her tone that she could not control. "And Urse's mate can't be there. We already know John provokes the response. If he's there, this won't work."

"Yeah, I know," Gus replied, shaking his head. "So, I think we should just try this with Mellie, first." He sighed. "Or maybe, test first with Peter, to see if he triggers you because there's no way Peter is letting his mate go into danger without being present."

Laura understood the issue. Mated pairs were fiercely protective of each other. The men would not—could not—let their women face possible danger. Laura knew wolves were that way, and apparently, so were bears. She wasn't sure the witch women felt the same protective urges, but if these were true matings, they would understand their bear shifter mates' need to shield them. That didn't make this situation any easier, but Laura definitely understood.

"How do you want to do this?" she asked, knowing Gus and the others must have come up with some sort of strategy.

CHAPTER 14

"We're going to clear the street. I'll walk you downstairs, and Mellie will be waiting on the porch," Gus told her. "Peter will be in front of the building. We figure you'll see him first, and if you're triggered, we can get a good look at what happens. Mellie can dive off the end of the porch to safety, and Peter is a big son of a gun with a lot of magic. He can probably survive whatever you might throw at him, if the worst should happen."

"But, once I'm triggered, I might just keep going. There might not be an *off* button," she said carefully, giving voice to what had recently become her greatest fear.

"I think I have a solution for that, as well," Gus replied solemnly, though she noticed he didn't go into detail about his so-called *solution*. "None of us really think that's likely to happen. The mages who had you had enough time to tailor the compulsions so that they wouldn't show if a target wasn't in sight. We're betting that they'd have taken the time and effort to make sure their sleeper agent—you—was not *switched on*, for lack of a better term, all the time and easily taken out. They probably figured you could hit a target, then go dormant to strike another again, later."

She thought about that for a moment in light of what she remembered of the people who had held her. They were devious enough, that was for sure, to plan something like that as a failsafe in case she ever should escape. The vile creatures they were, they wouldn't want to just let her go. No, better to make her into a weapon. As if they hadn't already visited enough horror on her existence.

Hell—if you believed in such a place—was too good for those bastards who had taken so much from her. If she ever got the chance, she would end them. Each and every one of them. Once and for all. No afterlife. No chance of coming back in any form. She wanted their energy dissipated to the farthest realms and beyond, where it could never recombine to harm anyone ever again.

If such things were possible. She'd had a lot of time to think about a just punishment for the people who had dared to hold her captive for so long. She'd daydreamed in her delirium of what she wanted to do to them. What she wanted to happen to them. Eventually, the bloodthirstiness of her wolf had given way to the more rational plans of her human side. She didn't just want to hurt those mages. She wanted to end them permanently. For all time.

It was her fondest wish.

But, to do that, she needed to be rid of the compulsions they had placed upon her. And, to accomplish that seemingly impossible task, she had to take a few risks. Of course, the risk wasn't hers alone. Everyone who tried to help her was facing a risk of one kind or another, as well. That they were willing to do so for her—a relative stranger in town—spoke volumes about the people of Grizzly Cove and their integrity.

"If they're willing to take the risk…" she thought aloud. She straightened her spine and blinked, refocusing on Gus's beloved face. "I think you're on to something. There's a very good chance that they would have designed the compulsions in such a way. The mages who had me… They weren't just garden variety bad guys. They were highly placed and very powerful. As time went along, and nobody could take any more from me because I'd learned to hide in the fey realm, I got passed along to protégés. They were of less importance but were being groomed for bigger things. They were all very powerful and very conniving, if a bit young and unproven. I can see them currying favor with their elders by crafting all kinds of surprises—including the compulsions placed on me, in case I escaped."

Gus was nodding. "It seems logical," he agreed. "So, if you're up for this, we'd like to try it after dinner. Mellie needs to see what's going on with you, if she can, so she can work on the right potion, or combination of potions, to at least get started counteracting what was done. Everyone agrees that there are probably layers to what they put on you because you were under their control for so long, and there were so many different mages involved in your captivity. Each one probably tinkered with different spells and bindings."

"That sounds about right. I could feel it…sometimes. In the beginning, I felt everything, but after I fled to the fey realm, I only felt occasional twinges that told me they were trying things. I didn't really want to know what they were doing." She sighed. "Perhaps that was cowardly of me. It certainly seems foolish now."

Gus placed one hand over hers on the countertop. "If there's one thing you are not, it's a coward. No one I know could have held up half as well as you did for so long. And, you should know, some of us have dealt with captivity. Lesser duration, of course, but still captivity with all the uncertainties around being rescued or being able to escape. I know what I'm talking about."

That meant a lot, coming from him. She turned her hand over under his and clasped his fingers, squeezing gently. She couldn't find the words to express what she was feeling, but she thought he understood.

Gus set everything up after dinner had been consumed and everyone was ready. Unbeknownst to Laura, others would be watching her besides just Mellie. Urse would be there, out of sight, but ready to observe and assist, should it become necessary. John would be with her.

Mellie had volunteered to be the focus of this test, to draw fire, if need be. She was a brave woman. And her mate was going nuts, but he understood her need to help. Peter would leap into action to protect his mate, if need be. They were going to do this test as safely as possible, but there would still be some risk to all involved.

Gus would be behind Laura, ready to take her down to the ground, if he had to. He wanted to be the one to tackle her. Nobody else would be as gentle, and he just couldn't take the idea of anyone else touching her right now. Not when their mating was so delicately balanced and dependent on the outcome of this crisis.

Gus's inner bear was a lot calmer, usually, than the other guys he knew, but in this situation, even the spirit bear was getting agitated. The bear wanted this over with so Gus could gather his mate in his arms and hold her close all night long. He wanted to cosset her and make love to her as gently as he knew how, then do it all over again...wild. He wanted to show her how much he cared for her, but they'd have to get through this trial first. And then, they'd have to get through more trials as they worked through this problem.

They had to be able to fix this. They just *had* to. Gus would accept no other outcome.

"Are you about ready?" Gus asked Laura as he got off the phone.

Gus had coordinated with Peter, who was coordinating with everyone else. Peter, Mellie's mate, was Gus's only point of contact because they all were well aware how good wolf hearing was. Peter and Gus had worked out a code that Laura wouldn't be able to interpret. From the few words they'd exchanged, Gus knew that everyone was in place on the street and in various protected vantage points. Anyone who could sense magic was going to be watching Laura, not just Mellie.

After whatever happened...happened...if everyone was all right, the magic circle would meet to discuss what they'd all observed. Gus would take charge of Laura. The plan was that he would stay with her for the rest of the night, and in the morning, if all went as planned, Marilee would spell him, spending time with her mother in the apartment, while Gus met with the magic circle and the leadership of the town to figure out what form their next steps would take.

Laura stood by the door to the apartment, shifting from foot to foot nervously. Gus went over to her and put his arms around her, rocking her gently, hoping to calm her. The fact that she snuggled into his embrace was gratifying, and it settled his bear side a bit. *Good mate.*

"Are you sure you want to do this? We can cancel and try to figure another way," he offered, not knowing what other way there could be, but if Laura really couldn't handle this, he'd move heaven and earth to find one.

She pulled back a bit to look up into his eyes. "It's okay. I can do it. I'm just...scared."

"I have a confession," he told her in a gentle voice. "I am, too."

She smiled, as he'd hoped she would. "Now, that, I find hard to believe. Nothing scares the spirit bear." She let him go and moved closer to the door. "Let's do this, before I lose my nerve."

Gus escorted Laura out of the apartment and down the stairs. The groundwork had been laid by others. The whole town, just about, was in on this mission, and everyone was off the streets, under cover and prepared. Gus had been in on the planning. He knew, for example, that there were at least two snipers on the roofs of buildings across the street, armed with powerful tranquilizer rounds. Nobody was willing to pretend that the tranquilizers would be one hundred percent effective against magical compulsions, but it was worth a try if the worst should happen.

The team on the ground was suited up like they used to be in their commando days. Tactical radios were in every ear, and most were wearing dark camouflage to blend in more with their surroundings. Night was starting to fall, so the twilight helped mask those that hid in the shadows. They would need every advantage to help in this situation. Nobody wanted anyone to get hurt—be it town folk or Laura. The best result they could hope for was to gather enough information to help Laura without anyone taking damage on either side.

Laura took a deep breath as they approached the door that would lead to the porch and then the street. She couldn't see anyone through any of the windows, which she counted as a blessing. She was trusting Gus, and the rest of the townspeople, to have prepared properly, so as to limit any damage if she went all *atom bomb* in the middle of Main Street.

She paused a few steps from the door to collect herself. Something inside was telling her to give up. To not go outside. To not confront this problem head on, which was her usual way of dealing with things in her life. Or, *it had been*, until she'd spent years in captivity.

Whatever was trying to stop her now, it wasn't part of her. It was something that had been *done to* her. No way would Laura stand for that. She wouldn't be bullied. She wouldn't be cowed. She wouldn't be made to feel fear or antipathy that wasn't rightfully hers. No way. No how.

She closed her eyes, took a deep breath and walked the few steps up to the door, placing her hands upon the push bar that would open it to the outside. Now or never.

"Are we ready?" she asked Gus in a voice that shook only a little.

"All set," he replied quickly, in that dark, rumbly voice that she loved so much. The fear that she would never hear that voice again was real, but she wouldn't let it stop her from doing what she had to do… What was right.

"Let's do this."

She pushed open the door, stepped over the threshold, then opened her eyes.

The first thing she saw was a big man. Peter. She'd met him once, in passing. He was Babushka's grandson. Russian. With dragon shifter blood in his ancestry. Highly magical.

All of these thoughts flashed through her conscious mind

while somewhere in her subconscious, something dark and sinister was stirring. It recognized Peter as a force for good. A highly magical shifter with no recognition patterns.

What?

Laura shook her head at the odd thought. Recognition patterns? What the heck? She tucked away that thought for later consideration as she felt physically ill. Retching a bit as an evil wave spread up from her core, trying to spill out of her body, she felt magic behind it. Not *her* magic, though it coaxed a magical response from that part of her being. It corrupted her magic into something dangerous. Something that could very well be deadly.

"Look out!" she screamed as the wave broke, spilling out into the street, toward Peter. She doubled over as the wave pulled out her own energy with it. Damn. That hurt!

She watched from streaming eyes as Peter didn't move. Why wasn't he moving? Did the silly bear think he could withstand that wave of malevolent energy? Dammit! *Move, man, move!*

But he stayed put.

As Laura watched in horror, time seemed to slow. Everything happened at a snail's pace. She felt the magic ripped out of her being and watched helplessly as it headed for Peter, like a malicious arrow, aimed straight for his heart.

The crazy bear-man stood his ground with no change of expression on his face. He looked mildly interested, and a tad defiant. Cocky son of a gun. As the arrow of dark energy approached him, Laura wanted desperately to shut her eyes and not look at what would happen to Peter—an innocent in all of this, after all. But she couldn't do it. She had to see the result of her unconscious actions. To look away would be cowardly. It would dishonor Peter's bravery and sacrifice in setting himself up as the target in a shooting match where nobody in this town knew the rules.

Only the bad guys knew what would happen if and when Laura's compulsions were triggered. They'd set them up. They'd designed them. They were the puppet masters in this demented show. How she would like to sink her teeth into them. Give them back just a little of the pain they were causing her, those she loved, and the innocent people of this town, who had shown her nothing but kindness.

The wave shot forward. In reality, Laura knew it was traveling in the blink of an eye, but she saw it go as if in super slow motion. It got within a few feet of Peter and then... It hit something. Something clear that turned opaque with the energy as it absorbed it and took it into itself.

A shield? Oh, thank the Goddess!

Someone had put a ward around Peter. Probably Urse, Laura realized, as the power inside her built again. She sent up a fervent prayer that the barrier could take another round because, like it or not, it was going to happen.

This time, when the power ripped out of her, it made her hands rise and twin fire bolts shot from her clenched fists, aimed right at Peter. Damn. That was just awful, but she had literally *no* control over what was happening with her body.

The shield held. It captured her energy and drained it away, into the ground. Harmless.

But it took longer to dissipate. The ward was weakening. Would it withstand a third attack?

Laura was drained, but she could feel something inside her trying to regroup and gather more strength, even as her spirit revolted against it and fought to maintain its own power. She would *not* be used in such a way again.

"Seen enough?" Gus's voice floated over her as if she was down some deep well.

She looked up just enough to see Mellie's horrified face at one end of the porch. The magic rose and wanted to strike out at her, but Laura was through being used. She fought it. Tooth and claw, her inner wolf fought against the compulsion.

"Get me out of here," she growled at Gus, just barely able to hang on as the power tried to build up enough again to strike out. "Now." She hoped he understood the urgency of her wolf's growl.

"She's fighting it." Marilee's voice came to Laura from the other side of the porch and sent a cooling shock over her singed senses. Her daughter. Her baby. She would *not* let the evil magic anywhere near her child.

Laura was still doubled over, but she felt Gus's arms slide around her middle, and she didn't fight. She let him haul her backwards through the still-open door to the building.

Thank heaven. He was taking her at her word and using his greater strength to pull her away from danger. Not danger to her—but the danger that she posed to everyone outside. Everyone, except Marilee, of course.

Laura was grateful that the guesses of the magic circle had been correct. She felt the compulsion winding down inside her as the targets were removed. Or, rather, as she was removed from the targets. With any luck, she would revert to the state she'd been in before. A coiled spring, ready to strike when the opportunity arose.

She just had to keep herself away from the opportunities.

She had to go back to being a prisoner within her own apartment.

Laura wanted to rage at the unfairness of it all, but she was too tired. As the energies pulled back and wound down, she was left limp and depressed all over again. Drained. Which was a relief, actually. She'd been so worried that, once triggered fully, she wouldn't be able to revert back to her un-triggered state. They would've had to put her down if that was the case. She couldn't have lived long in that condition.

Gus didn't let go of her once, for which she was grateful. He lifted her in his strong arms and carried her up the stairs and back into her apartment. Only then, did he let her go, placing her on the couch with a gentle touch and sitting down beside her.

"That was some firepower," he said, smiling at her. Why was he smiling at her? Hadn't he just seen her try to kill one of his friends? "So... Do you feel like blasting me?"

"No," she answered weakly.

Her wolf half was tired from fighting the power, but the

power didn't want to rise against Gus. Perhaps it knew she would never hurt Gus. She'd kill herself before she hurt him.

"That's good," he replied, still smiling. "Looked like you calmed down when you saw Marilee, too. Don't want to blast her either, I bet."

Laura shook her head tiredly. "No. I could never hurt my baby."

"The ones who crafted the spells to control your magic probably knew that and left a workaround to keep you viable as a sleeper agent," Gus observed. He sounded cool now. Almost clinical. She couldn't understand why he wasn't more upset with her.

She'd loosed terrible magics against his friend. Magics she didn't even know she could command, to be honest. It wasn't natural for a shifter to have that kind of firepower. Then again, she'd always lived as a shifter, but she had fey blood. She'd utilized that connection to escape her captors, as much as she could. She shouldn't be surprised that they'd figured it out and used her ancestry against her.

Somehow, they'd tapped into that hidden part of her and roused something she never would have otherwise detected. They'd found power inside her that could come out—though it hurt like a bitch. When that magic had ripped out of her, she'd felt something tear loose inside, and she almost believed that a rift had been created that would never be sealed. And, oh, how it had *hurt*.

"I don't think I'm ever going to be the same after today," she whispered, trembling in the aftermath.

"You won't. You'll be stronger," he assured her. "When you survive this, you'll be more than you were before."

She turned to look at him, nonplussed. "How could you know that?"

"It's the strongest theory of the many we've batted around about you," he admitted with a slight shrug. "But, more than that, it's something I feel. An instinct. Intuition, if you will." He paused, considering her. "I'm seldom wrong when I have this kind of feeling," he told her in a low, steady voice that made her want to hope he was right.

"Shifters don't do magic," she insisted quietly.

"Some do," he said, surprising her. "You might end up being one of them. But first, we have to see how this all plays out. Mellie and Urse got a good look at what happened down there just now. So did Sabrina and Marilee. They were watching your aura and the power that rose in you. They're comparing notes, even as we speak, and I'm sure they're going to come up with a strategy to help fix this. They won't rest until they have a solution. You can be sure of that."

CHAPTER 15

Gus had been unprepared for the harsh reality of what he had just seen. He hadn't thought it would be quite that bad, or that powerful. Oh, he knew Laura had some fey blood somewhere back in her ancestry, but he hadn't thought it would manifest quite so intensely. That had been some real power she'd been throwing out there, in the middle of Main Street.

He didn't want to let on to her just how shocked he'd been. Luckily, as a shaman, he'd had years to perfect his poker face. People often told him things that would shock others, seeking his help with various problems in their lives. He couldn't react negatively when people trusted him with their deepest secrets. He couldn't really react in any way at all. He'd learned to just take it in and let it flow over him, so he wouldn't betray his inner thoughts in a way that might jeopardize his ability to help the person revealing themselves so deeply to him.

Gus used that skill, now. It was clear that Laura was depressed enough as it was. He didn't want to add to her burden. It was hard enough to counteract the lethargy—or whatever it was—that had been added to the layers of spells cast upon her. That lethargy seemed cruelly designed to stop her from doing anything about her situation, once she became aware of it. It was likely meant to make her wallow in self-pity and depression so that she wouldn't seek help or even try to help herself.

Gus was having none of that. He was happy to see that when push came to shove, Laura had fought against it. She wasn't a normally passive person, and her captors must have realized that. They'd done what they could to subdue her normal warrior reaction—and they'd succeeded to some extent. She was definitely looking glum to Gus's eyes, but she was also braver than she realized, and he knew even this kind of magic wouldn't hold her down long.

She had already begun to break the depression's hold. He would point out to her that she'd held off releasing a third volley of magical energy through what had looked to him like a Herculean effort. She'd managed, though, which had to be counted as a victory. And not just a small victory. No, that had been a real accomplishment.

There was a knock on the door, followed immediately by a familiar voice. "Mama? It's me. Marilee."

Gus looked at Laura as he rose from the couch. "You okay to see her?" he asked gently, fully prepared to run interference if he had to, even between mother and child.

Laura nodded tightly. "I couldn't hurt her, even when the magic was high. You two are probably the only two people in this town that are safe around me right now."

She looked so forlorn, he really wanted to go over and give her a hug. Marilee was tapping on the door again, though, so it would have to wait. At least, for a little while.

Gus went over and opened the door, letting the younger woman in. Marilee didn't waste any time. She ran right over to her mother and took her into that hug that Gus had wanted to provide, without hesitation. It was a bit of a marvel. Marilee was often a very timid little wolf, but she'd been learning to stand on her own two feet since mating with King. He supported her, encouraging her. It was a good match, and a true mating, and slowly, Marilee was starting to come into her own.

"Are you okay? How do you feel?" Marilee asked her mother, breaking off the hug to hold Laura at arm's length and get a good look at her.

"Tired," Laura answered. "Kind of wrung out."

"It hurt when the magic ripped out of you, didn't it?" Marilee asked quietly, her tone solemn and concerned. "I saw it. Your aura changed."

"It hurt," Laura confirmed, her expression grim. "It hurt a lot."

Marilee hugged Laura again, rubbing her back with a reassuring hand. "I'm so sorry," Marilee crooned, offering comfort, "but we learned so much." Her tone grew more excited, and she drew back, again, to look at Laura and Gus. "Everybody is meeting, right now, to discuss everything, but I wanted to come check on you, first. Urse and Mellie both seemed really positive that they could do something to break a lot of the spells laid on you. They wanted me to tell you that it'll probably be tomorrow morning before they're ready to try anything. For one thing, they want you to rest and recuperate. A lot of that magical energy came right out of your being, Urse said. She thinks you need to eat and sleep, in that order, so you'll be ready in the morning to fight against the spells, while Urse and Mellie try to break them in various ways. They're going to work through the night on different strategies, I think."

"Please tell them both—tell all of them—that I'm very grateful for their efforts on my behalf. And please…apologize to Peter. I really didn't want to blast him." Laura cringed. "I feel just awful about that."

Marilee laughed. "Oh, don't worry about him. I heard him laughing with Mellie and talking about how much fun it was." Marilee shook her head. "I'm not sure I'll ever get used to the way these bears think. My mate thinks fighting six guys at one time was just a warm up, and he didn't even blink when the final two guys pulled guns on him." Marilee shook her head.

Gus laughed at her reaction. "Ladies, the things we saw in the service probably make us a little different than most other people—even shifters. Some of the stuff that went down was pretty insane," he admitted, shaking his head. "I served with Peter, and he always had a berserker streak. We still tease him about it." Gus sat down in the chair at a right angle to the couch the women shared. "If anyone would find facing down mage bolts of uncertain strength *fun*, it's him."

Marilee bounced up from her seat on the couch and smiled lovingly at her mother. "I just came to make sure you were okay. I'm going to go back and listen in on what they all saw and what they're planning. If there are any major changes, I'll call...or...well...I'm sure the guys will keep Gus informed. I know they have better communications options." She winked at Gus, and he had to laugh. Her mate had probably been telling her all about their tac radios and hand signals. Special Forces teams all had many unique ways of communicating important information without using civilian channels or devices. "Oh! I forgot," Marilee exclaimed as her cell phone buzzed in her jeans pocket. She reached back for it and headed for the door. "Nell, Ash and Tina sent food over from the bakery with King. I'm going to meet him at the stairs and bring it in, then I'll get out of your hair."

"Please, thank them all for me," Laura said in a subdued tone. She looked...haggard. That was the only word for her depleted condition. Laura leaned her head back to rest on the top of the couch and closed her eyes.

Marilee sent Gus a worried look, but he tried to reassure her with his calm expression. It seemed to work as she took one last glance at her mother then fled out of the apartment to fetch the food delivery. She was back in less than a minute and put the bags on the kitchen island, then went to the couch to give her mother another hug and kiss.

"Call me if you need me," she said, then looked up at Gus until he nodded. "Try not to worry," she said softly to her mother. "Everyone wants to make this better. I won't accept any other outcome."

That got a small chuckle out of Laura as she sat up straighter on the couch and looked at her daughter with loving, but sad eyes. "That may not be possible, sweetie. It's not completely under our control."

Marilee's expression became fierce. "It will be," she promised, leaning forward to kiss her cheek again, before getting up and leaving the apartment.

She closed the door behind her, and Gus got up to lock it, just in case. While it wasn't truly necessary to lock doors in Grizzly Cove, in this case, the more obstacles between anyone accidentally encountering Laura in her current state, the better. Of course, locking the door from this side was meant more as a reminder to anyone who might be on the other side of the door that the place was off-limits, for now.

Everybody knew that, so Gus's gesture was more symbolic than anything. He was locking the world out, not necessarily locking Laura in. She had the ability to turn the latch and leave, but she wouldn't. Not unless there was some further component to the spells laid on her by her captors that he didn't yet know about. But that was highly unlikely, and Gus would be with her at all times. He wasn't about to let her out of his sight for a moment. He cared too much about what happened to her.

They had admitted their love to one another, but they hadn't taken that final leap to the topic of a mating between them. Gus had never been mated, so he didn't know exactly what to expect, but he thought privately—and had for a while now—that Laura was his one true mate. For her part, Gus knew that Laura was very confused about what she'd thought had been a true mating between herself and Marilee's father, Roger, the human mage.

The very fact that Gus believed Laura to be his mate negated the validity of that prior, so-called, mating. They'd talked about it a bit, but no decisions or declarations had been made. Gus had wanted to give Laura time to come to grips with all the new information. He knew it had to hurt her to think that she'd either deluded herself or been bamboozled by Roger into believing that he was her true mate.

With everything that had happened to Laura recently, he'd

wanted to give her space to really think things through before he put her on the spot and asked her to share the rest of her life with him. He knew in his heart that they were meant to be together. He just had to time it right so that she was in a place emotionally that she could not only accept that—accept him—but welcome a new mate into her life.

It would be another big adjustment in a string of them that had hit Laura lately. Gus was trying to be patient, but sleeping with her…making love with her…wasn't enough to satisfy his soul. He wanted the commitment, the surety that mating would give them both. His inner bear demanded it, and that grouchy grizzly was growing ever more impatient to claim his pretty white wolf for all time.

Gus and Laura shared the thick sandwiches that the Baker sisters had sent over. Gus was gratified to see Laura eat an entire sandwich and some chips. Her strength had been depleted by the confrontation, and she would need the calories to help repair any damage done to the inner fabric of her being. Sleep was the other thing she needed. Desperately.

When she finished with her sandwich, and her eyes started drifting closed right there at the table, Gus picked her up in his arms and carried her to the bedroom. He helped her undress and tucked her in before leaving the bedroom to quickly tidy up the food and put the leftovers in the fridge. She might wake in the middle of the night and want a midnight snack. It would be a shame to let the food spoil when it would come in handy later.

After cleaning up and setting up coffee for the morning, Gus rejoined Laura in the bedroom. She was sound asleep and didn't wake when he climbed beneath the covers with her. He would hold her through the night and pray for a good outcome tomorrow.

Laura woke sometime later. It felt like hours had passed, and judging from the lack of even the faintest light filtering in through the window, it was sometime in the middle of the night. A quick glance at the bedside clock told her it was a little after three in the morning. She took stock, silently, lying in bed, staring up at the ceiling. She still felt groggy, but a slight buzzing in the background of her mind wouldn't allow her to go back to sleep. Not at the moment, anyway.

Slowly, she moved her legs over the side of the bed. She had a robe by her feet on top of the covers, where she habitually kept it. She reached for it, gratified to find it was still there. She wrapped herself in its soft silkiness and got up. She knew there was probably no way to rise from the bed without also waking Gus, but it couldn't be helped. She couldn't stay there any longer. The quiet and darkness was getting to her. She needed light and color. She needed to see for herself that she wasn't still in a dark box, unable to leave.

Silently, she padded out into the living area on bare feet. She was aware of Gus and the rustling of the sheets behind her as she left the bedroom, but he followed at a slower pace, which didn't seem threatening. He wasn't her jailor. He was, instead, a companion, his calm presence expressing, without words, his concern for her safety and well-being. She was okay with that. More than *okay*, if truth be told. She loved having him show her in so many unspoken ways that he truly did love her.

The more that happened to them—and the more he stayed beside her, helping, not hemming her in emotionally, though she had no other choice than to keep herself physically separate from the rest of the townsfolk—the more she felt his love. He was such a good man. Such a supportive partner. She would have been within her rights to not trust the declarations of love they had both made. She'd been burned before by a man who spoke of love.

But, with Gus, it was all different. Her wariness couldn't stand in the face of his silent, supportive presence. He was there for her in a way that Roger never had been. Laura could feel Gus's care and concern with every fiber of her being. Now that she thought back on it, she hadn't ever felt that with Roger.

She was almost convinced at this point that Roger had

duped her, somehow. Or, maybe, in her eagerness to find a mate, she had done it to herself. Or, perhaps, it was some combination of the two. Whatever had happened way back then, she would never regret having Marilee, though she could wish the last twenty years in captivity had never happened.

Laura went into the kitchen and got herself a cool glass of water. That was a good place to start in banishing the demons that had come to visit her sleep. Cold, pure water, whenever she wanted it, was a luxury after the years when her captors doled out drugged potions and nasty-tasting water from human municipal systems that had all sorts of chemicals in it. The Grizzly Cove water was of the highest quality. Pure and fresh from nearby mountain springs on land the town owned and piped directly to the inhabitants of the cove. Yum.

"You hungry?" Gus asked in a low rumble as he stepped into the kitchen and moved directly to the refrigerator.

He opened it, reached in and pulled out a plate of sandwiches left over from earlier, she imagined. She'd been a little too woozy to remember exactly what had transpired before she fell asleep, but she did remember sandwiches at some point.

"Yeah, I could go for one of those," she told him, refilling her water glass at the sink.

Gus put the plate on the kitchen island and turned to retrieve plates from one of the cabinets. He set them on the island, one for each of them, then let her make first choice from the available sandwiches on the platter. She picked a ham and cheese on some kind of rustic bread with a crunchy crust and put it on her plate. She noticed Gus took half of each of the two sandwiches that were left, and she found it endearing. Could he not choose between the two, so he took a little of both?

"I won't be able to eat more than this, so you could have both of those if you're hungry," she told him. She could feel a faint smile curving her lips, and she realized it was Gus that had made her smile when, just a little bit ago, she'd thought she'd never smile again.

"Honey, never ask a bear if he's hungry because the answer will always—and I mean *always*—be yes." He grinned at her as he put the halves he'd taken back on the platter and just picked up the platter, instead of using the smaller plate. "You could have some of this if you want." He offered the platter to her again. "Before I eat it all."

She chuckled with him and declined. "No, you eat it. This will hold me until breakfast or maybe even lunch. I'm still not used to eating like a normal person yet, and even before, I didn't eat as much as the other wolves. They blamed that on my fey blood, too. I got teased a lot for eating like a human."

She wandered over to the windows, but it was the empty easel on the table there that was her goal. She had a number of blank canvases left, and although artificial light wasn't the best for painting, she wasn't picky. Right now, she needed color and expression. Her fingers literally itched to paint.

"Do you mind if I..." she asked, gesturing toward the painting area she'd set up on the side table.

"Go right ahead," Gus told her, moving around to sit on the couch with his platter.

Laura took a few bites of her sandwich while she set up a new canvas and prepared her paints and brushes. Once she started painting, her focus narrowed. She took the occasional nibble of her food while contemplating the image she was creating, but by and large, the rest of her sandwich sat, ignored, on her plate.

She painted fast and furious, sliding color over color, mixing in sweeping strokes to make new tints and effects. She knew just what she wanted to portray and was pleased with the results, as she went along. She was aware of Gus in a peripheral way, sitting on the couch, working steadily through his pile of sandwiches. She didn't mind. The painting was paramount, at the moment. Something she felt compelled to complete.

But it wasn't the compulsion of the evil that had been done to her. No, this was the compulsion she had only recently rediscovered. The healthy one that pushed an artist to keep going. To create. To express themselves in the medium of their choice and put their inner vision out into the world. She considered it a healthy drive, that was healing to her soul.

CHAPTER 16

Gus polished off the sandwiches but didn't move from the couch. Not for a good long while. He wanted to give Laura the time she apparently needed to put her feelings into images. He sensed the act of painting was both cathartic and therapeutic at this moment. She'd felt driven enough to leave the bedroom so that she could capture whatever images had disturbed her sleep. The late-night nosh hadn't really been her idea, or her main objective. He had seen that easily enough.

But providing sustenance to the woman he loved was imperative for his wild side. His inner bear wanted to feed her. She was so skinny. Not yet fully recovered from the years of starvation and deprivation she had suffered. His inner bear was going nuts trying to protect her, nourish her and make sure she had the time and space to recover fully. It was quite possibly the most important thing in his existence at the moment.

That was a big change. Gus had always been at the center of the unit—now the town. He'd been concerned for all of his friends and their well-being. Now, while he still cared about the guys and their lives, his focus had shifted so that *the* most important person in his life was Laura. He wasn't used to having just one person be the sole focus of his energies. He'd half-convinced himself that it was because she had been so badly abused, but now that they had acknowledged their love for each other, he suspected it was something much deeper.

He was thinking *mate* almost constantly, now. The urge to claim that exclusive relationship and have her admit that she believed in it, too, was nearly all-consuming. But he couldn't rush her. He knew he had to finesse this situation. To rush her might scare her off, and he didn't want that. Not in a million years. He would apply no pressure. Would use no guile. She'd had enough of that in the past, if his suspicions were correct about Roger. No, this time, if she chose to accept Gus as her mate, it would be done freely and without any question in either of their minds.

When it looked like her painting frenzy was winding down, Gus got up and took the now-empty platter to the sink. He rinsed the few things that were in there before loading them into the dishwasher. He'd run the dishwasher tomorrow. For tonight, it was enough just to tidy up the place while Laura finished her art while she nibbled on the remains of her ham and cheese.

She was sort of absently eating while she looked at her canvas. He couldn't see it from his vantage point. He hadn't tried to peek at it before she was done, but it looked like she was slowing down, now. Just making minor corrections and tiny brush strokes, here and there, after staring at it for a bit. He figured it was close to done, and he was interested to get a look at what had consumed her so.

He walked quietly around to approach from behind. He didn't want to disturb her concentration, so he approached slowly, making the occasional sound that would register in her subconscious. She would know that he was creeping up on her, but the fact that he allowed her to hear him would signal no danger.

He was glad he took the subtle route when he got his first good look at the painting. It was a small canvas, but he recognized the bear at the center of a maelstrom of energy lines, at once. The burgundy fur was a dead giveaway. She had painted a Kamchatka bear. Peter, in fact, though Gus didn't think she'd ever seen Pete in bear form. Maybe Babushka had shared photos. Or maybe Laura's gift for painting was more magical than they realized. This wasn't the first time she had painted something she had never seen in person accurately.

"What are all the lines of color?" Gus asked gently as he paused beside her.

"Magic swirls. Aura glow. Ward ripples," she replied, speaking each word slowly, as if she was only just realizing what she had painted and was having trouble putting it into words. "It's a gift for Peter, to apologize," she told Gus gently as she finally put down her brush and began cleaning up. She worked silently, for a moment, before looking up at Gus. "Do you think he'll like it?"

"Honey," Gus told her, placing one arm around her shoulder as she stood, "he's going to love it. You made him look even bigger than he already is. That boy has a massive ego, and this is going to stroke it, I have no doubt." Gus grinned as he looked at the image of the giant burgundy bear holding its own in the midst of waves of color and light.

Magical energies in every variety—good, evil, and in between—surrounded him. Yeah, Peter was going to hang that picture where he could gloat over it and remind everybody who saw it about the day he'd stood up to a volley of mage bolts right there on Main Street. Gus could only grin and shake his head.

Laura stretched and yawned hugely. Gus took that as his cue. "Anything else you need to do about the brushes and paints?" he asked, not wanting to cause her trouble later by neglecting her tools now, but she shook her head.

"All taken care of," she told him as she stood up. She collected her plate and walked over to the sink to drop it in.

"Leave that for later. Right now," he told her, closing in from behind and wrapping his arms around her waist as he placed nibbling kisses on the side of her neck, "I've got other plans."

"Oh, you do, do you?" she replied, a playful note in her voice that let him know she wasn't uninterested in a little sexy fun before going back to sleep.

"I do," he said in a low voice, turning her in his arms so that her butt rested against the countertop. He lifted her easily to sit on the polished granite, and he stepped between her spread thighs as if he belonged there.

Which he did. He most definitely did.

Laura lifted her arms to settle around his shoulders, tugging him closer so that she could match her lips to his. He was such a good kisser. He lit her up from within with just a little nibble of his lips and the swish of his tongue in the right places. Damn.

She wanted more, and she didn't want to wait. Laura was pushing at his clothing with impatient hands, and Gus seemed to get a clue about what she wanted from him. He stepped back for just a moment to tear his T-shirt over his head, then he was back, all hard muscles and warm skin. Mm. He felt so good under her hands.

But she wanted still more. She fused her lips to his and tangled their tongues together in a delicate duel. She put her arms around his shoulders again, and drew him close.

That's what she'd wanted. The feel of his hard-muscled chest against her. He was so warm. So big because... Well, he *was* a bear. Even in his human form, he was a big man. Most werewolf males were larger than human males but tended to be lithely muscular. Tall and rangy, for the most part. She had dabbled with some of the young men in her Pack as a girl, as did most younger folk. But the man she'd chosen and *thought* was her mate had been human.

Roger had been tall and in very good shape, but his musculature had been nothing like a werewolf male. She didn't even bother comparing him to Gus. There really was just no comparison. She was fast realizing that there was nothing quite as big, cuddly, massively muscular, or protective as a werebear.

And, at this moment, it seemed nothing quite as impatient. She felt the same. Laura was able to push his jeans down around his hips before he growled and lifted her clear off the counter for a moment while he swept her robe off completely. He thoughtfully put the discarded clothing on the granite before setting her back down. She could deal with denim against her bare ass, but cold granite might've been a shock too far.

When he had her back on the counter, he wasted no time positioning himself between her thighs once more. Only this time, there was no barrier of cloth keeping them apart. He looked into her eyes as he moved closer, sliding deeply into her core.

"All right?" he asked as he joined her fully, his dark eyes flashing with desire held in check. He was the most thoughtful lover she'd ever had the good fortune to be with.

Laura nodded, unable to form words. Gus grinned—a sexy upturn of one corner of his mouth—as he started to move by slow increments. Barely discernible pulses began a rhythm that soon had her panting with need.

He took her on a slow, sexy ride that brought her a whole new awareness of her body and her needs as a woman. Only now did she realize how little Roger had tried to meet those needs. She came in Gus's embrace, but he didn't join her. Not yet. He ran his fingers over her back and praised her in a way that would make her blush at any other time, then he brought her to a new level of passion with the strokes of both his hands and his cock, deep inside her.

When she came again, he joined her, holding her tight to his body as they both spasmed in joy and ardent relief. Gus swept her into his arms, supporting her with both hands under her ass as he walked with her into the bedroom.

He separated from her only long enough to go into the bathroom. She heard the sounds of running water and closed her eyes as she lay on the bed. The next thing she knew, he was back, a warm, wet washcloth between her thighs as he washed her clean, taking special care to excite her, all over again, with the new sensations.

"Are you trying to kill me?" she asked him, only half joking.

Gus chuckled, and even that deep sound was a turn on at that moment. "Nope," he replied, the smile still in his tone. "Just trying to drive you wild, if that's all right with you."

"Mm." She rolled over to face him as the washcloth left her body. She opened her eyes and met his gaze as he sat on the side of the bed. "It's more than all right, as you have probably already guessed."

"Well, in that case..." Gus got on his knees as he positioned her on her back once more. He took up a position between her legs, but he was too far down the bed.

Or was he? Surely, he didn't mean to...?

A moment later, she found out that he surely did as his mouth closed over her clit and sucked gently, sending her senses skyrocketing upwards. Sweet Mother of All! The man had a true talent for bringing females pleasure. This one, in particular.

He rode her through the first climax, holding her hips down with both hands while she tried to buck as her body went into spasms of pleasure. When that passed, he tried different tactics involving his tongue and fingers until she screamed his name as she came again. His masculine chuckle drifted down to her as he repositioned himself to join with her, once again.

She wasn't sure she could take much more, but then, he slid into her, and she realized she would take whatever he wanted to dish out. She was quickly becoming addicted to him and the amazing passion he roused in her. She wouldn't be surprised if, after this time with him, she would be ruined for any other man.

As he pushed her higher, yet again, she realized she didn't care. Being with Gus was special. Almost sacred. He had shown her, in no uncertain terms, that her life had not ended when she'd lost Roger. Or when she'd been held prisoner for so long. No. Her life went on, and she was still, blessedly, alive. Gus proved that to her beyond the shadow of a doubt with his tender, passionate, wild lovemaking.

With all the uncertainty surrounding her, that single fact was clear as crystal. She sent a prayer to the Goddess in thanks for this time. This man. This amazing affirmation that her life wasn't over.

She'd been so very afraid for so long, but with Gus's gentle coaxing, she was realizing that the fear was unnecessary. She was alive. Truly alive, in his arms.

Everything else would work out. Somehow.

She hoped.

Fear had turned to hope, and Gus had done that for her. It was fragile. It was new. But it was there. A tiny seedling needing to be nurtured. Something that just might blossom if given enough care and attention.

CHAPTER 17

Marilee was in the kitchen when Laura shuffled in the next morning, still yawning from the delicious lack of sleep of the night before. Lee Lee had brought breakfast and more supplies from the bakery and was busy stocking the fridge when Laura walked in. Gus was making coffee for himself, but he quickly diverted the cup he was fixing for himself and gave it to Laura with a peck on the cheek. He was a good person to have around in the morning when Laura couldn't quite open her eyes without a little caffeine boost.

She nodded her thanks at him as she sipped the reviving brew. Marilee popped out from behind the door of the refrigerator and came over to give Laura a good morning hug. She looked happy, despite the situation—the magical problem Laura still had and the rather obvious possessiveness Gus was displaying.

Laura hadn't really talked to Marilee about Gus. At least, not in a definitive way. She thought Marilee approved of the increasing closeness between Laura and Gus, but at some point, they probably should sit down and talk about it, if Laura was going to stay here…and stay with Gus.

Right now, she couldn't see the path ahead. If she stayed in Grizzly Cove—and that was a big *if*—she would definitely want to be with Gus. But, if they couldn't find a solution to her problem, then all bets were off, and she'd have to figure out some other path. Or no path at all. Death was always still an option.

But she wouldn't go quietly. No, Laura had a plan if nothing else could be done. She'd go hunt down those *Venifucus* bastards and take out a few of them when she went. She *owed* them that...and a whole lot more. She lay awake at night dreaming, sometimes, about taking her revenge.

Which reminded her of something...

"I wonder if there's a way I can record more of the information I remember about the various mages and minions I knew, just in case..." She didn't finish the sentence. Gus and Marilee were both looking at her. Marilee's expression was stricken, and Gus just looked grim.

Laura shook her head and went over to the island where breakfast was laid out. Fluffy rolls from the bakery and bacon and eggs still hot from the pan. Gus must have cooked to supplement the bakery delivery. Laura helped herself to a plate full and then sat down and began eating. Neither Gus nor Marilee had commented on her statement, and she wouldn't look at them.

She probably shouldn't have said anything, but she'd just been thinking out loud. She would make further notes about the *Venifucus* agents she'd seen and been tortured by over the years when she had time. She wanted to give the good guys as much information as possible, so that, if they couldn't find a solution for her, at least someone would have the data and be able to go after the evil beings that visited such pain and suffering on the world. Someone needed to get those guys. She only wished it could be her, but she knew a one-woman vendetta wouldn't get too far against such powerful evil.

After a few moments, Marilee and Gus joined Laura at the table, plates of their own in front of them. They ate together for a few moments, taking the edge off their hunger, before Marilee spoke.

"King is with the others, helping set things up," Marilee told them in between bites. "Mellie has a potion that should suppress all your magic for about an hour. If you're willing to take it, Urse thinks—if it works—she can do some work on unraveling some of the magics that were laid on you. We all got a good look at the surface of what was compelling you, and Urse thinks it's similar to the bindings that were on the box they were transporting you in. She was able to break those pretty easily, it looked like, so I think she'll definitely be able to do *something* if you're willing to try this scheme." Marilee looked so earnest Laura couldn't refuse her.

"I'll try just about anything as long as there's not too much danger to the people around me. I don't want to hurt anyone," Laura said, measuring her words carefully. She *really* didn't want to hurt anyone who was only trying to help her.

"They want to do it outside. Urse said something about dispersing the energy into Mother Earth and sparing any buildings in case something rips loose that can't be contained." Marilee cringed a little but forged ahead. "They don't want to waste too much time because the potion should only affect you for a limited time, so transporting you to the stone circle is probably not feasible. So, Mellie suggested the beach behind this building. It's already a no-go zone for the duration, and it's close. Once the potion takes effect, you can just come out the back door, and Urse and John will be there, ready."

"John?" Laura frowned. She *really* didn't want to take any potshots at the Alpha bear if she could help it.

"Yeah, it's the only way he'd let Urse try this. He's *uber*-protective of her. Just like all the other mated guys."

Marilee's silly grin was easy to interpret. She was thinking about her own mate and how protective he was of her. Laura felt a little pang. She was so happy her daughter had found such happiness, but it made it that much clearer that Laura's first mating—though she figured that wasn't the right word for it, now—hadn't been true.

"So, the idea is that you'll see John first, and if he triggers your mad super-villain skills, he'll be ready for you, like Peter was. But, if the potion does its job, Urse will start doing her thing and keep going until the potion starts to wear off or you're free. Whichever happens first." Marilee shrugged, but it was clear she knew the import of what she was saying.

"It can't be that simple," Laura cautioned them all.

"It probably won't be," Gus said in somber tones. "But, if it works, it'll be a good start."

And that's how, a few hours later, Laura found herself being escorted to the seldom-used back door of Gus's building, which opened onto a small, gated pathway that led to the beach. Gus and Laura paused before the door, waiting for Marilee. She was bringing the potion that Laura would drink immediately before going outside.

Laura stepped closer to Gus, needing a bit of reassurance. She wasn't normally so needy, but her emotions were in tatters with the magic working on her psyche, as well as her magical core. She needed a hug, and Gus didn't disappoint. All she had to do was step closer and put her arms out, and he swept her into his embrace.

Bear hugs were the best. Laura immediately felt the comfort and warmth radiating off him in waves of love. She could actually *feel* the love in the way he touched her. She'd never felt that before. Not with any of the boys she'd known before Roger, or with Roger, himself. Her supposed mate. She knew for certain, now, after being with Gus, that Roger hadn't been hers. Not the way he should have been.

A little pang made her scrunch her eyes shut. She'd lost so much time because of a foolish conviction. Whether she'd been manipulated or merely foolish, she still wasn't sure, but either way, it was a blow. Laura had always thought she'd been so strong. Everyone in her Pack had thought her one of the tough gals. An Alpha bitch. Sure of herself and her place in the world.

She'd been a fool.

Laura sighed, shaking her head as she stepped back from Gus's embrace. She could hear Marilee entering the building. Before her daughter got to them, there was one thing she wanted to tell Gus, just in case this all went wrong.

"I've just realized something for sure... Roger wasn't my mate." All the sadness she felt at learning that awful truth was negated by the shock and dawning wonder in Gus's eyes.

She wasn't ready to take this to the logical next step. Not yet. Not until she was sure she *had* a future to plan. But she owed Gus the truth, and she could see her admission made him happy. At least she could give him that. For now.

Marilee rushed over to them, brandishing a small brown glass bottle. She had a nervous smile on her face, and Laura knew her time in this condition was up. Whether or not she'd be freed totally of the magics was a long shot, but whatever happened next, Laura was hopeful that her burden would be a little lighter than it was right now... If she survived.

Marilee handed over the bottle then impulsively gave Laura a quick hug. "It'll be okay," she said on an emotion-filled whisper. She cleared her throat before speaking again, as she let Laura go. "Mellie says to down all in a quick gulp then head outside. The dampening effects should be pretty much immediate."

Laura unscrewed the little cap on the bottle and took an experimental sniff. It didn't smell bad. In fact, it might not taste all that bad either—but there was only one way to find out. She looked from Marilee to Gus, and then, holding Gus's gaze, she quickly tilted the bottle to her lips and swallowed down the contents.

She'd been right. It wasn't vile. It wasn't exactly soda pop either, but it wasn't bad tasting. It fizzed along her senses, a little like pop, but not in her digestive tract. No, this effect was along her the magical pathways where power flowed in her being. She'd never been more aware of them until this moment.

"Wow," she said, trying to follow the sensations in her being without much success. "I feel weird."

"Good weird or bad weird?" Gus wanted to know. His eyes narrowed as he looked at her.

"It's good," Marilee said, smiling. "I can see the change in her energy. It's…it's like it's clouded or something. Dampened. Just like Mellie said." Marilee put her hand on Laura's shoulder. "You need to go outside."

Laura let them lead her out. Gus opened the door and preceded them down the path, letting Marilee escort Laura, who felt a bit dazed. It was like she was looking at the world through a filter. A hazy film between her and the rest of reality. She didn't feel drugged…exactly. She just felt a bit like her senses were wrapped in cotton. Fuzzy.

Gus gave a piercing whistle and shouted, "Heads up," as they walked down the little path.

When Gus moved aside, she saw John waiting for her at the end of the little pathway that was bounded on either side by a dune garden. She felt the magic wanting to rise within her, but…

It was blocked. Blessed relief tore through her, and she felt tears rolling down her cheeks.

"It wants to get at him, but it can't," she whispered. Gus heard and reported back.

"All clear," he told John.

The Alpha bear still looked skeptical, but he moved aside to reveal his mate standing behind him. Urse was already scrutinizing Laura with a knowing look on her face.

Gus moved to Laura's side as she set foot out of the little gate and onto the beach. Marilee was on her right, Gus on her left.

"How are you holding up?" Gus asked in a low voice.

"It's fighting to get out, but so far, it can't," she reported. "Tell them to work fast, though. It's not the most…uh…comfortable feeling in the world." And that's all she would say about the pain. She could endure a little pain if it meant being freed of this encumbrance.

Gus's eyes narrowed. He seemed to understand more than she wanted to let on, but he nodded with a grim cast to his handsome features. Even now, the love she felt for him made things a little bit easier. He was there for her in ways that Roger had never been. Through thick and thin. The few good times they'd had and the horrible bad things that had been happening all around her. If she got out of this even remotely well, she'd do all in her power to keep him. Forever.

But she wouldn't take that final step until she was sure she would survive. She couldn't do that to Gus. If she acknowledged a mating between them, she'd be setting him up for a life of sorrow if she didn't make it through this. He didn't deserve that. Gus was nothing but kind. She couldn't ruin his life the way Roger and all that had happened to her had ruined her life thus far.

As she looked at Gus's beloved face, she felt something tear loose and drop away. She jumped, realizing Urse had been hard at work while Laura had been woolgathering. She turned wide eyes to the *strega*.

Urse was so focused on her task, she probably didn't even see Laura looking at her, but Laura thought she sensed a little quick of Urse's lips upward. A tiny grin for a tiny triumph? Laura thought so.

"One of the bands of power just dropped away," Marilee told them. "The energy was absorbed into the sand at your feet, Mama. It looked just like when Urse took the bands off the box they had you in."

"I felt something tear and drop away," Laura told her daughter in wonder. "This is actually working." Laura didn't want to get her hopes up too high.

The *Venifucus* mages had had years to work on her. Logically, it made sense that it would take more than a few minutes to un-do all that had been done. Frankly, Laura hadn't been altogether certain that Urse would be able to do *anything*, but there was proof, now. Laura could feel the lightening of the load of magic on her, though she hadn't really been aware of it, in that way, before now.

As the minutes wore on, Laura could feel each binding come loose as Urse cut through it with her own, more powerful spells. At one point, Laura staggered under the impact as a particularly dense knot of magic came loose and drained away. Gus was there to catch her, grabbing the arm she had flung out to steady herself.

He didn't let go but supported her through the rest of the ordeal. It hurt like hell when Urse's counter-spells sawed through the energy bands that had been wrapped around Laura so tightly, they felt like part of the fabric of her soul. Each time Urse succeeded in breaking through one of the bonds, Laura felt like a red-hot poker had seared the skin of her inner being. Her wolf sat through it, growling inside her skull.

It endured the pain stoically, understanding, on some basic level, that it was necessary. As each magical constraint came loose, the wolf gave off a little victory howl inside, where only Laura could hear it. The wolf was right. Each little victory was worth celebrating, but her human half was flagging. It didn't have the endurance of the wolf.

And now...the magic was gathering, and it really felt like it was going to tear loose and hurt someone, this time. Laura grasped at Gus's hand.

"They have to hurry. I think the potion is wearing off. I can feel it gathering. Malevolent. Wanting to hurt. To kill." She gasped as more pain ripped through her—the good spells Urse was casting meeting resistance now, from the bad things that had been wrapped around her. "Tell them to go!" she shouted at Gus, sobbing as her body was overcome, and both Gus and Marilee were repulsed by a wave of...something.

She was aware of them being pushed to either side, but she was riding a bucking bronco, and she didn't have time or strength to worry. Not then. It was John the power inside her wanted. It was John who was her target. And the witch he protected.

Aw, shit!

Twin bolts of dark energy flowed out of her hands and left her trembling. She fell to her knees gasping for breath as pain blacked out her vision for a moment. She was sobbing. Wrung out. Oh, sweet Mother of All, what had she done?

Laura blinked open her streaming eyes to see what had happened. She had to know. Had she killed them both?

But Urse and John were still standing. Blessed be! Urse had a look of consternation on her face, her lips twisted in a frown. "Well, that's all for today, I suppose," she said rather nonchalantly, Laura thought, after being attacked by mage bolts.

Thankfully, before the power could gather again, both Urse and John left the beach. As soon as they were out of sight, the urgency that had been building depleted itself. The come down left Laura limp on the ground.

Gus picked her up and carried her back into the building, Marilee trailing along with them, opening and closing doors on their path. They were quiet until they reached the apartment. Marilee went into the kitchen area and began brewing a tea blend that Mellie had sent along for after, but Gus sat with Laura on the couch and just held her while she shook in the aftermath.

Laura just sat there for a while, taking stock. Everything ached. She felt bruised from the inside out. But there was one thing that felt very different. One thing that gave her hope. She turned in Gus's arms to look up at his beloved face.

"You know," she told him quietly, "there's something good that has come out of this. I'm not depressed anymore."

"You're not?" Gus asked gently, stroking her hair. "That's good."

"Yeah, it is," she agreed, starting to feel a bit more like her old self. "I'm not depressed. I'm angry. Really, really angry at the people who did this to me. If I ever get the chance, I would hunt every single one of them and kill them all."

She heard the growl in her own voice, knowing it was the wolf's instincts that made her so bloodthirsty. She didn't mind. That was how it was supposed to be. She was a werewolf. Not a mouse. More than that, she was an Alpha bitch in her prime.

It was about time she reclaimed that part of her identity. It was about time to become the hunter, instead of the prey.

CHAPTER 18

Gus wasn't surprised by Laura's words. He was a predator too. He knew that the bear spirit he carried inside was much more pragmatic than his human half. Regardless, both halves of his soul wanted the mages who had hurt Laura so badly destroyed. Utterly and completely. Wiped from the face of the earth and their spirits torn to shreds, never to reform.

Marilee had left after giving her mother the tea Mellie had sent along. She would be the go-between, they had decided, that would bring word back and forth. Gus could get phone and text updates, but for some of the more complicated details, it was just easier to have Marilee go talk to people and bring back their opinions. She was also useful as a courier, as she had been this morning.

Hours had passed since that breakfast they had all shared together. Hours during which Gus had been made to stand by and watch Laura put through the wringer. He knew she'd been in a lot of pain. She hadn't shown it much outwardly, but he'd seen it. She was a brave, brave woman. Brave, brave *mate*, his inner bear insisted.

But she had to acknowledge the mating. Without her agreement, it would all be one-sided. Forever.

The tea, he was glad to note, did have some calming properties. Laura fell into a doze, which was probably the best thing for her at the moment. Gus sat beside her, his arm around her shoulders as she snuggled into him. She had kicked off her shoes and curled her feet up onto the couch so that she was in a near-fetal position as she rested against his chest.

He just held her, trying to impart some of his strength to her battered spirit. She was such a good woman, he wished there was more that he could do to ease the burden she carried. As it was, all he could do was just be there for her.

Marilee returned at lunchtime with take-out from the restaurant. The town was certainly taking good care of Laura. Gus would definitely thank Zak and his mate for their care—as well as the Baker sisters and their mates—when this was all over. Perhaps he could throw a party for everyone where he did all the cooking. Oh, how he'd love that to be a *mating* celebration, but he knew he'd have to wait for Laura to come around and realize that they were *true* mates. So unlike the so-called mate she'd believed she'd had before.

Marilee brought lunch and news. Laura woke when Gus left the couch to open the door for Marilee and seemed to be feeling better as she sat at the table and absently dabbled with one of her carvings. Marilee and Gus got to work setting the food out and making up plates while Marilee filled them in on what everyone had said after the morning's work.

"Urse says she just got the top layer of spells and that there are a lot more underneath, but she's confident she can do more to cut through them," Marilee told them as she worked. "Mellie promised to keep working on her potions, as well. She's trying to find something that will last longer, as well as something that might help break some of the layers of compulsion all at once, which would be a lot simpler and probably easier on you, Mama." Marilee frowned as she went over to the table and set a plate in front of her mother. "Did it hurt a lot? It looked pretty bad from where I was standing."

Laura just shook her head. "It hurt," she said finally, after a moment's pause, "but I'm still standing."

Just barely, Gus thought, but he didn't say it aloud.

"Well, they were all happy with this first attempt. Urse said she got through a lot more of it than she thought she would. She's willing to try the same thing tomorrow, if you're up for it. She says the layers she could see were all very similar and should respond to the same strategy. She wants to get down to the more complex layers of spells and see what they're made of, but the other stuff is in the way and has to be dealt with first."

Laura sighed. "Yeah, we can do it again tomorrow. I'm willing."

Marilee smiled. "Good. I'll tell them. But don't be surprised if they find a better way. They're all still working and comparing notes. They're good people, Mama, and they don't really want to hurt you any more than they have to."

Laura reached over to pat her daughter's hand, resting on the table as she sat beside her. "I know. Please thank them for their efforts. I'm glad I ended up here where at least they're willing to try to help me. I shudder to think what might've happened if I'd been loosed somewhere else."

"You think that was their plan?" Gus asked, not liking the direction of Laura's suggestion.

She nodded slowly. "I think, if they could wake me up, they were going to send me out as a weapon," she said quietly. "They were after Marilee because they thought she would be able to get to me when nothing else they tried could. They were right about that. She was the only reason I came out of the coma-like state I'd put myself in. But, if they had captured her and made that happen without the benefit of all the good people of Grizzly Cove on watch to help, I shudder to think of the results."

They would've used her as a weapon, Gus realized. Someone compelled to kill other shifters and magical folk, against her own wishes. A true sleeper agent who didn't even know what she'd been sent to do until it happened.

"They figured they weren't going to get my power," Laura went on, shrugging. "They wanted to get something out of their investment in me, even if it was only to take some of our people out with me when I finally went supernova."

Grim thoughts crowded Gus's mind. He wasn't surprised that Laura had only just put the pieces together. Perhaps some of the magic done to her—like that spell that made her depressed and lethargic, and unlikely to seek help—had also been meant to cloud her memories. Now that some of that was gone, she might be remembering more.

They spent the day quietly. Marilee left after lunch, and Gus stayed with Laura. She was so tired and so obviously still hurting in her soul from what she'd been through that morning. He contacted John and the other guys via text and email. He'd brought his laptop over from his place and sat working quietly while Laura painted or carved.

He brought her more of Mellie's tea, which helped for short periods of time with the spirit pain, but Gus knew from his shamanic training that some hurts, only time could heal fully. He was there for her, supporting her in whatever way she needed him, but the insult done to her spirit had been done over a period of decades. It wasn't going to be healed overnight.

Still, it hurt him to see her hurting. He sent out email after email to the guys in town, as well as contacts he'd made over the years. He had already sought advice from some trusted advisors over the past days, and now, he took the time to bring them up to speed on the efforts they'd made so far and the results.

He even reached out to the High Priestess, Bettina. It was rumored that she was part fey. Perhaps she would have some insight into helping a shifter of mixed heritage. He sat there, sending out his messages like arrows, waiting for the replies. As they came in, there was little good news. For most of his friends, this situation was a bit out of their depth.

The one bit of good news came later in the day when the High Priestess responded. She didn't give him advice in the email but told him she would call John and his mate directly and talk the situation over with them. That was good. If anyone could describe the magical problem accurately, it was Urse, and Gus supposed the High Priestess was observing proper protocol in contacting the Alpha of the Clan before offering her advice.

Marilee tapped on the apartment door after dinner and passed along another item that lifted Laura's spirits visibly. Apparently, Nansee, the leader of the mer pod, had sent her best wishes and a box full of things from the ocean that she thought Laura might be able to use in her art. The thoughtful gift and the message Nansee had sent with them—that the mer of Grizzly Cove wished her well and hoped she would be better soon—definitely brought a happy tear to Laura's eye.

Gus was glad Laura had made friends among the people of the cove. It couldn't hurt to have the powerful leader of the local mer pod on your side.

After Marilee had left for the night, Gus and Laura sat quietly, much as they had done during the afternoon. She was working on art and enjoying looking through the box of goodies Nansee had sent while Gus stewed and communicated with his friends electronically about the situation. He was urging them to try to find some alternative to what they'd done this morning because it was obvious to him that Laura was still in a great deal of pain, even if she refused to admit the full extent of it.

"Is that email?" Laura asked as they sat at opposite ends of the table. "What you're doing on the computer," she clarified. She had missed so much technology during her long captivity.

"Yeah," he admitted, leaning back in his chair and rubbing a hand through his hair.

"Who are you talking to?" She kept working on her carving but seemed interested in making small talk for the first time since that morning.

"Just the guys. We're kicking around ideas," he told her, not wanting to get too specific.

She put her tools down and looked at him steadily. "Normally, you'd be doing that in person, right?"

He couldn't lie to her. "Yeah, probably," he admitted.

"I'm sorry you're stuck babysitting," she said, looking studiously down at her work.

Gus frowned. He typed a final message to his buddies and closed the computer. "That's it," he said with finality as he stood up. He walked over to her and took her by the hand, tugging gently upward until she stood in front of him. "I'm not sorry at all that I'm *stuck*, as you put it, looking after the woman I love. So, just get that thought right out of your head this minute." He pulled her into his arms and just held her gently, rocking slightly, back and forth. "I love you, Laura." His words were whispered near her ear as he held her tight. "I always want to be with you, regardless of the circumstances."

He knew his words were skating very close to the idea of being mates, but maybe it was time she started thinking about it. He didn't want to push her into anything, but he also wanted her to know, without doubt, that he was here, ready and waiting should she decide she wanted to take things to the next level with him.

"I like being with you, too," she whispered back. His heart sank a little, but he didn't let it show. He'd wanted more, but she wasn't ready. He didn't know what he'd do if she never crossed that line from lover to mate, but he knew one thing for sure—he'd never abandon her.

"Come on," he said, moving so that only one arm was around her shoulders as they both faced the same way. He started walking, and she followed. "Let's call it a night."

She didn't object, and they went into the bedroom together. He proceeded to make love to her as gently as he knew how. He wanted to show her without words how much he cared for her. He wanted her to understand that he was there for her in every possible way. That he loved her more than anything in this world, or any other.

They came together slow, moving gently in a rhythm as old as time.

When they both came down from a delicious high, they lay together, bodies intertwined as their breathing slowed. All barriers were down, for the moment. Emotions were very close to the surface, but still, he sensed her holding back.

Gus rubbed slow circles over her shoulder, just trying to be there for her. Trying to show without words that he supported her in whatever way she needed.

"You all right?" he asked.

"Better," she replied in a satisfied whisper. She was silent a moment, then she cuddled closer. "I guess I wasn't fooling you at all, huh? About how much what they did this morning hurt me?"

He shook his head slightly. "Nah. I knew you were in pain. You were so brave, Laura. So strong."

"That's just it," she replied, tucking her chin into his chest, not meeting his eyes. "I honestly don't know if I can handle another session like that one. I feel so...bruised. Battered, really. On the inside, where it doesn't show but hurts even more." She paused while he felt every one of her words like a strike to his own soul. It had been worse than he'd suspected. "I don't know if I'm strong enough." Her words faded to a barely-there whisper as she shivered.

Gus tucked her close to him and brought the blanket up over them both with his free hand. It was time to tell her a few things.

"First of all, you are the strongest being I know—and that includes all my military friends. We've all been through trials, but nothing like what you endured. You are a proven warrior, Laura, so don't ever doubt yourself. Second, I've already been talking to folks about changing the approach. I didn't like what that first session did to you. I knew you were in pain, even though you hid the full extent of it. Now, I'm doubly glad I started working on an alternate plan." He paused as she looked up at him in surprise.

He kissed her. He couldn't help himself. She was just so lovely. When he pulled back, her gaze was soft, again. Relaxed. Good.

"What did you do?" she asked, proving she hadn't forgotten what he'd been saying.

"Remember all that email I was sending and receiving?" She nodded against his chest. "I reached out to an expert outside Grizzly Cove."

"Who?" her question was a breath of sound.

"I contacted the High Priestess, Bettina. They say she has fey blood. I thought she might have a better understanding of you, and your ancestry, and how that might affect what we're trying to do," he told her.

Laura was very still. "What did she say?"

"She got right back to me, but she said she was going to contact John and Urse directly since that's really the proper protocol. I sort of went over John's head, but I know he won't mind too much. We're bears, not wolves. We're not that big on hierarchy to begin with." Gus shrugged slightly. "Plus, being a shaman gives me a lot of leeway in spiritual, and sometimes magical, matters. What's happening to you is a bit of both, I think."

"Do you know what happened? Did the High Priestess talk to them yet?"

"She did. She contacted them right away, and the last I heard, they were devising a new strategy. Urse asked me to pass along an apology to you because Bettina seemed to think that her approach was wrong for someone of your background and might damage you." Gus frowned, but let his anger over the situation go. They should've been talking to Bettina from the start. "They're devising something in concert with the High Priestess to account for your hybrid nature. You're a mix of human, mage, wolf, and fey, and you've recently spent a lot of time with your spirit on the edges of the fey realm. Bettina thinks that changed you on a fundamental level and made your magic stronger. The fact that you were also sort of *absent* from your body when the *Venifucus* mages were doing their worst to you, means that the spells they wove are closer to your spiritual center than they would have been had you been actively fighting them. That means it'll take a more delicate approach to break them."

"I guess that makes sense," Laura said quietly, as if she

was thinking through his words very carefully.

"The straight-on human way Urse was using will work, up to a point, Bettina said, but it's more damaging because it's like sawing through a cord with a blunt knife. What they were talking about when I called it a night sounded much more elegant and high-level," he told her. "Urse sounded like she was drinking in the information from the High Priestess, and more than willing to learn whatever she needed to learn in order to minimize the trauma to you. She felt really bad after Bettina pointed out how the work she'd done so far must've affected you, and she's really sorry."

"It's okay. It's not like she did it on purpose," Laura allowed generously.

"Still, I suspect she will be apologizing in person, once it's safe to do so." And, if not, Gus would make sure he put the bug in Urse's ear that an apology was the least she owed Laura for putting her though such an ordeal when there were better alternatives she hadn't thought to explore.

"Do you really think it'll ever be safe?" Laura asked, a bit of gloom in her tone that Gus didn't like. He squeezed her close, offering the warmth and comfort of his body in the shifter way.

"I believe it will happen," he told her simply. "I refuse to believe in any other outcome."

CHAPTER 19

Gus felt a bit grim about the plan the others had come up with while he'd been sleeping. The High Priestess had apparently counselled them to force a crisis. She insisted that it would go easier on Laura all around, if they let her loose all the magic she could call, thereby depleting herself. Once her magical reserves were gone, they could go in and perform the delicate magical *surgery* that should remove the remainder of the compulsions all at one time.

No matter how much they made the case that doing this all at once would minimize the trauma to Laura, Gus couldn't find a way to be happy about it. They'd come up with a plan—as he'd asked them to do—but he wasn't sure it was a *better* plan than the one they'd started with. The only thing that made him go along with this crazy idea was that it had the High Priestess's input and blessing. Gus wouldn't have let them do it otherwise.

He drove her to the stone circle that wasn't far from his own land. Main Street had been cleared so they could drive out of town without incident. So far, so good.

The team that had been working on this new approach overnight had decided to use the natural shielding of the henge to help in the confrontation that was to come. The idea was to get Laura into the circle of stones. Urse would then

179

add a ward around the stones, adding to its natural protections and preventing Laura's magic from escaping the stone circle. That wasn't something just every mage could do, but with Urse's special talent for ward casting, it could be done with a minimum of power drain on her.

That was important because she would need all her skill and strength to do the next part...

"Doing all right?" Gus asked Laura as they pulled over. He parked on the grass near the standing stones. He couldn't see anyone, but he knew they were around. Downwind, if they were smart, or Laura's sensitive wolf nose would scent them.

Laura took a deep breath and gave Gus a tight smile. "Let's just get this over with."

Gus nodded, keeping his grim thoughts to himself. He'd explained everything to Laura over a light breakfast. He'd read her the pertinent parts of the email, and Marilee had come to talk over a few things Urse wanted Laura to know about how this plan would go down. They weren't telling Laura everything, because nobody knew how much of the compulsion would be influenced by her conscious thoughts.

They got out of Gus's truck and walked, hand-in-hand, into the stone circle. Gus felt a deep sense of relief that he'd been able to get her this far without incident.

"So...we just wait here?" Laura asked, seeming a bit uncomfortable.

"Shouldn't be long now," he said, squeezing her hand in reassurance. "I think Urse is going to ward the circle. Ah. There it is." Gus sensed a faint shimmer to the air around the stones.

Urse had put up one of her strongest wards. It would contain any magic inside the circle, using the strength of the stones themselves to power it. That would leave Urse free to use her magic to break the compulsions using the new knowledge Bettina had given her.

Laura jerked around, looking all over for some unseen enemy.

"You okay?" Gus asked, concerned. This behavior was

new.

"It's building," she told him on a gasp. "It wants a target. It knows it's being stalked."

"Damn." Gus didn't like this. Not one bit. But he was committed to seeing this through, even if watching how much it hurt her killed him by slow degrees.

John suddenly stepped out from behind one of the standing stones on the far side of the circle from where they'd entered. Laura saw him, and her hand rose, throwing a magical fireball right at him. John didn't even duck. He was outside the ring, and the power of Laura's magic didn't hit him. Rather, it was absorbed by the ward and sank into the stones, pouring down into the earth, neutralized.

Rather than launch another volley at John, Laura withheld her fire. Perhaps the compulsions were learning not to waste energy once a target was out of reach. It didn't matter because they had more than one target to present.

Peter was the next one to step out from behind a standing stone. Laura grunted, and both hands rose as if against her will to loose mage fire in his direction. Once again, the power went into the ward and the stone nearest it absorbed the energy and put it down into the ground, out of reach.

Laura growled, her wolf not happy with any of this. Gus knew how she felt. He hated watching her be controlled by something placed on her by evil people. He could see how it hurt her. And drained her.

The latter was what they were hoping for. They needed to deplete her energy before Urse could do the real work of the day.

Brody stepped out from behind another stone, and Laura immediately opened fire with mage energy. It was deflected and redirected. Zak was next, and Laura responded in kind, though it was clear her energy was dropping. Still, she had quite a bit left, if Gus was any judge.

King took the next mage bolt, and his brother, Ace, the following one. Each was a little weaker, but still would have been something to consider, had there not been the ward and stones keeping them all safe.

"Gus!" Laura gasped as she dropped to her knees.

He could see she was in a lot of pain, but he was powerless to make it stop. This had to be done if they were going to be able to help her. They had to drain all her power away and work while she was depleted. There was no other way. Or so, the High Priestess had assured them.

Gus sank down beside her and tried to take her into his arms, but her skin was charged with energy. He was actually shocked by the contact and pushed away. He tried again, but had the same result.

"Honey, I'm going to go bear. Lean against me. I'll support you." He met her gaze as he quickly shucked his clothing.

He held her gaze throughout the shift to his bear form, and when he approached her, this time, the energy crackled along his fur and dissipated. He was able to touch her.

Gus snugged right up against her side, hoping she would loop one of her arms around his neck, but her control was wrenched away as John stepped into the space between the standing stones, taunting her. Laura's hand shot out, and lightning leaped from her fingers to be absorbed into the ward and sizzle along the stones into the ground.

When she drooped, Gus was there to support her. Her left arm draped over his body as she turned into him, but there was still magic sizzling through her. He could feel it singeing his fur in places, but he didn't care. Whatever he was experiencing, it was nothing to the pain she had to be feeling.

It was brutal. Gus almost couldn't bear to watch as his lover self-destructed. One by one, the men of Grizzly Cove moved closer, as John had done, provoking a response. She could only raise her right hand, and each volley of power was a little weaker than the last, until…

She flamed out.

There was no other way to describe the phenomenon. Gus saw that last bit of magical energy flicker, then die. She was tapped out.

The others saw it, too.

"Clear?" John asked, still at the perimeter of the circle.

Laura passed out as the last of her energy drained away, and Gus quickly shifted to his human form so he could catch her in his arms. He lifted her, carrying her to the altar slab at the center of the circle of stones. He placed her upon it as gently as he possibly could.

"She's out," he told his friends and brothers-in-arms.

John stepped into the circle first, and walked cautiously closer. When nothing happened, he gave the signal for the other men to advance. When Laura made no move at all, the men closed the circle around her. Gus stayed with her as the other six joined him.

"Is it safe for the women?" John asked, but his question became superfluous as Urse marched right out from behind the stone John had been behind and jogged up to the altar. John rolled his eyes. "Honey, did I give you the signal?"

Urse pushed past him. "We're wasting valuable time while I wait for your signal, J. We've got to do as much as possible before she regains power and starts blasting again." Urse was examining Laura as she elbowed her way closer, through the circle of men. "We don't want to do this to her over and over. Too much strain on her spirit and body could kill her. If we do this right, once will be enough. At most, twice. Just give me some space."

She said no more as John gave the nod and the men backed away. Only Gus remained with Laura. Nothing and no one would keep him from her side. Not now. Not ever.

Urse worked her spell craft while Gus watched and prayed. He beseeched the Mother of All to protect Laura's spirit while the bonds of evil were removed from her being. He could actually feel the release of each of the compulsions as Urse did her thing. Something had changed drastically about the way she was approaching the magical bindings, and Gus felt sure that, with the High Priestess's help, Urse was on the right track.

As each evil spell broke, Laura's spirit grew lighter. She

seemed to be in less pain, not more. Yet, she was breaking free of the bonds that had weighed her down for so long.

"Bettina was right," Urse murmured at one point. "They tied a lot of this to her own power. This garbage was draining her to sustain itself." Urse made a face of disgust. "She ought to be a lot stronger without all this nonsense." Urse waved her hands a bit and spoke some words of human magic that were mumbled to Gus's hearing. It didn't matter. He trusted Urse to use her powers for good, as she had proven, over and over, she would.

"That's it for me," Urse said after a few minutes more when Gus had felt more of the bonds break to slither away into the altar. Harmless. The energy reabsorbed into the earth.

When Urse stepped back, Mellie came forward. She had a number of small bottles clanking in a small pouch. She took one out and used the dropper of the little bottle to place one drop of the potion on each of Laura's hands and feet, one over her heart and one on her forehead. Gus watched as the blueish potion disappeared into Laura's skin. He'd never seen anything like it before.

"What was that?"

"Just a little insurance," Mellie said with a twist of her lips. "Just in case she starts to wake up." She put that little vial back into her pouch and pulled out another. "Now, this one will work from the inside out," she murmured, placing a drop of pink liquid on Laura's lower lip. It slid into Laura's mouth as if it could move under its own power and disappeared.

The effect was visible. Laura's body began to glow with a cheerful pink tinge. Bubblegum pink. Happy pink. It was like looking at her through rose-colored glasses, only he wasn't wearing any glasses. When that faded, Gus could feel that, somehow, more of the bonds had been swept away with it.

Mellie repeated the anointing with a bright yellow—almost golden—concoction, this time, speaking some kind of incantation as she did her work. A few moments later, as the golden fluid seemed to spread over Laura's skin like a thin film, going under her clothing and over what seemed to be her entire body, a golden glow suffused her whole body, starting out a dark ochre and ramping up to the intensity of the sun, only without the heat. Laura's body actually lifted up a little off the stone altar as the golden shimmer dissipated straight upward, rising from her solar plexus and drawing off more of the malevolent magic with it as it left.

Laura sagged back against the altar when the light faded. But Mellie, apparently, wasn't done. She moved to stand at Laura's head and drew a thin line straight across her brow with a third, green potion, then covered the line with a large fresh leaf Gus recognized as a simple bay leaf.

"Let the laurel open your inner eye," Mellie muttered in English, just loud enough for Gus to hear. "Like the Oracles of Delphi, let it give you vision to help yourself," she continued. She interspersed the English with some Italian and even Latin words, plus some things that Gus couldn't make out, which were probably words of high magic that usually sounded muffled to non-mages.

The green leaf fluttered then pressed itself firmly to Laura's skin as a green glow started at her head and moved downward through her limbs and torso, to leech out through her fingertips and feet, directly into the living stone of the altar. More of the evil energy drained away with it.

This time, Mellie sagged after the work was complete. She held herself up with one hand on the altar, while she removed the bay leaf from Laura's forehead with the other. Her mate, Peter, was right behind her, and she leaned against him as he lifted his hand. It held a small, shiny copper bowl with ornate designs etched into the rim. Mellie placed the leaf, now dried and crackly where before it had been green and vibrant, into the bowl.

"Urse?" Mellie looked up at her sister. "Would you?"

Urse raised one hand, and the leaf in the ceremonial copper bowl went up in a little puff of flame. The smoke was green, not gray, and the flame itself was bright yellow with an aura of green around it.

Mellie closed her eyes briefly then looked at Gus. "That's all I can do for now. I just hope it's enough," she told him quietly.

"Thank you," Gus said, nodding gravely at Mellie before meeting Peter's gaze over her shoulder. Peter looked a little unhappy but resigned to the fact that his mate liked to help people. It was her calling as a *strega* witch.

Peter caught Mellie up in his arms and carried her away from the altar, taking her outside the circle of stones entirely. For all Gus knew, Peter took Mellie home. She had expended a great deal of her own energy in the potions and spells she'd cast here. Gus didn't blame Peter one bit for wanting to look after his mate. Gus would have done the same, had he been in Peter's shoes.

"Wow," Marilee said quietly. She had come up beside Gus as Peter had departed. "Mellie did something *huge*." Gus knew that Marilee could see magical auras under certain circumstances. He wasn't quite as gifted, but he could see some of what Mellie's potions had wrought, and he agreed. The little human potion witch had outdone herself.

"Mel's been growing. Ever since her success with warding the coast from the leviathan, she's gained in both confidence and ability," Urse said, coming up on Gus's other side.

They were facing the altar from the land side, the rocky beach and ocean beyond, just visible through the stones on the opposite side of the circle. Gus saw movement that caught his eye, and Urse sighed.

"Good," the Alpha female said, sounding relieved. "They're here."

The answer to who she was talking about was obvious as two women—mermaids, they had to be—walked up from the beach. They had donned quick coverings in the sarong style that covered the essentials. They must've had them stashed on shore somewhere or brought them in water-proof wrappers.

Gus knew one of the women. It was Nansee. The leader of the mer pod and the one who had befriended Laura to some extent. The woman beside her was someone Gus thought he'd seen around town once or twice, but he didn't know her name.

Gus gauged Laura's level of consciousness, and she was still down for the count. The expenditure of all her energy in the thwarted attacks, plus the drawing away of the bad energies by the spells and potions they'd used so far had combined to put her well under. They had a little more time to work before Gus would become concerned. For now, Laura's spirit was holding steady. That much, he was certain of. The spirit realm was his bailiwick as a shaman.

"I'm glad we made it in time," Nansee said as she approached. "How is she doing?"

Urse spoke for them all. "Holding steady. Mellie's potions did a lot of the work, but there are still some things left over from the *Venifucus* that we need to handle before she wakes up."

"This is Francis." Nansee gestured toward the other woman. This mermaid wasn't as robust looking as most of the others. She was smaller, almost petite, and she seemed shy. "Frannie, I'll introduce you to everyone more formally later. Right now, we've got work to do." Nansee smiled at her own words.

"I see that," Francis said softly, stepping closer to the altar. The ring of bear shifters had let the mermaids through, but Nansee held back and let her companion make the next move. Francis raised her hands over Laura's prone body and held them about a foot above her midsection, palms facing downward. "She is strong. Her spirit is pure, but it's clouded by the presence of…" Francis's head tilted to the side, and her eyes shut as she seemed to concentrate. "Evil laid on her soul," she said quietly, her eyes popping open. She looked back at Nansee. "It's just as you said." Her voice was pure and musical, like most of the mer that Gus had encountered.

"Can you help?" Urse asked gently.

Francis smiled, and Gus caught his breath. This little mermaid was, by far, the most enchanting member of her species Gus had ever encountered. And he meant that in the magical sense, not any sort of romantic way. She was clearly some sort of mer mage—or maybe she was their version of a priestess. He didn't know how the mer worked it, but this mermaid was very different from her sisters. He'd almost suspect she was at least part fey...

Which made total sense. The light began to dawn in his mind.

"Bettina sent you?" Gus asked Francis directly. The shy woman smiled up at him.

"When the High Priestess asks for a favor, I like to help out," Francis replied, grinning so that her dimples showed.

CHAPTER 20

From the light blonde hair flowing down her back to the bright blue eyes, bluer than the most tranquil lagoon, it was clear this mermaid was something more. With Francis's help, a lot more of the evil magic that had been laid on Laura's soul was taken away. When Urse took over working the active magics again, Francis watched over the entire operation, closing her eyes and communing with Laura on the spiritual plane.

Gus could see some of that, but the two women—Laura and Francis—were deeper. In the fey realm, perhaps? Or that *between* space that had safeguarded Laura before? He'd have to ask, later. For now, it was enough that Francis could see Laura's spirit and safeguard that precious essence while the last of the *Venifucus* magic was removed from her body.

When it was done, Francis smiled brightly. "I think that's it," she said, her musical voice reaching everyone in the circle. "She just needs to wake up."

"It's all gone?" Gus asked. "Are you sure?"

Francis nodded. "Her spirit is wholesome and unencumbered. I don't see anything from this side." Francis closed her eyes and seemed to search, then reopened them and smiled once more. "Yup. Pure and clean from the inside out."

189

Gus felt nearly overcome with relief. "I can't thank you enough," he said honestly. "I know Laura will want to thank you for your help, as well."

"She already has, in a way. She's still kind of unconscious, but she is aware on some level of what's going on. I feel her relief and gratitude. She has a pure spirit," Francis reported in a gentle tone, as if she was impressed by what she saw. "I didn't know land shifters could be so..." She seemed to realize what she was saying and blushed. "I mean..."

Nansee stepped forward and put her hand on Francis's shoulder. "Frannie doesn't come ashore much, but I'm trying to talk her into working part-time at one of the shops in your building," Nansee told Gus.

"You would be most welcome," Gus told Francis formally. "Laura is going to manage the building and the White Wolf Gallery, so you could get to know each other a bit more. I'm sure she'd like that. She doesn't have a lot of information about her fey heritage."

"Neither do I, really," Francis replied, "but I'd like to talk with Laura when she's feeling better," she replied softly, then moved back with Nansee, letting Urse take over once more.

"Let me just do my own little check," Urse said, then glanced over at Francis and Nansee. "No disrespect intended. It's just a formality."

Francis held up her hands, palms outward. "No offense taken. I understand. You can't be too careful with so many beings depending on your judgment."

Urse paused and smiled at Francis. "You do understand. Thank you."

She shook her head and focused once more, waving her hands over Laura from head to toe several times over. On the last pass, she began a soft chant, and though Gus couldn't make out the magical words, he felt the impact of the spell Urse was weaving. It was a protective spell. A personal ward. Urse was gifting Laura with something few people were ever given.

It was protection from anything like this ever happening

again. The ward Urse was crafting before Gus's astonished eyes would virtually guarantee that Laura could never have another person lay a malicious spell on her again. Not without some serious backlash.

When Urse was finished, she looked a bit drained, but John was there to support his mate. Gus just stared at her.

"Did you just do what I think you did?" he asked, unable to put the right combination of words together to describe what he thought he had just perceived.

"I gave her a special ward." Urse raised one hand to push back her hair, out of her face. "If anyone tries to put the whammy on her in the future, they're going to get it back, right in the teeth. It's a modified mirror ward. Something I cooked up especially for Laura."

Gus just shook his head at the generosity of spirit everyone had shown Laura. Especially Urse and her sister. They had really gone above and beyond.

"I bless the day the Mother of All brought you to our town," Gus said, with fervor. He would have said more, but Laura began to stir. All eyes went to her as Laura's eyes blinked open.

She squinted at Gus. "How'd we do?" she asked, sounding both groggy and cautious.

"You can't tell?" Gus grinned at her and helped her sit up on the low altar, supporting her with one arm around her shoulders. "It was a roaring success."

"It was?" Laura pushed her hair away from her eyes and took stock. Now that she thought about it, she felt lighter. Freer. Liberated, yet somehow protected.

"I hope you don't mind," Urse spoke up from where she stood leaning back against John's chest. He had both arms wrapped around his mate's middle. "I took the liberty of doing something, and I thought it would be easier to beg forgiveness than ask permission. I gave you a permanent, personal ward."

Laura wondered for a quick moment if the ward was for

her protection, or theirs? And she felt a little uncomfortable about someone putting yet *more* magic on her, when the goal had been to get it all off. Why had Urse done it? Shouldn't she have realized that, once free of the magical taint, Laura wouldn't want any more magic put on her?

"It's a type of mirror. So, if anyone ever tries to do anything to you, it'll reflect back on them. It won't be pleasant. And the worse their intent, the more it's going to hurt them," Urse said quietly. "I know I might've overstepped a bit, and I want you to know that I *can* take it off, if you want. I made it so that only I can remove it, just as a precaution in case you really didn't want it, but I thought…" Urse cleared her throat and forged ahead. "I thought it might ease your mind a little. You're protected now. Nobody should be able to cast evil on you, ever again."

"Urse's special gift is warding," Gus reminded Laura in a gentle tone. "If she says you're safe from now on, you are."

Tears came unbidden to Laura's eyes and flowed down her cheeks. This was the best gift anyone could have ever given her. She had lived with the fear that, even if they'd succeeded in freeing her of the compulsions, all it would take would be to get in range of a *Venifucus* mage, for the spellwork to be remade. She would have killed herself before she'd let that happen, but she was realistic enough to know that she might not get the chance. If the *Venifucus* got to her, she could easily become their weapon, all over again.

But, with Urse's gift, it couldn't happen. Laura was truly free.

"Thank you," she sobbed, relief overcoming her. "Thank you," she repeated, unable to say anything more as she cried quietly, overwhelmed for the moment. Gus stepped closer and took her into his arms, rocking her.

"You're safe. You're whole. You're free, my love," he told her. His words were the purest music to her ears. "And…" he whispered in her ear so that only she could hear, "…you're my mate. Aren't you?"

She pulled back to look into his eyes. This she could give

him. Finally. She could take the happiness and joy he offered and give it back to him to last a lifetime. Here, in this sacred place, in front of friends. She could be brave and do the right thing. For both of them.

"Yes, Gus. You're my mate, and I'm yours. For now. Forever."

*

After everyone heard that declaration, it didn't matter how tired they were, there was nothing for it but they must celebrate the new mating. Everybody piled into their vehicles and drove straight to Zak's. He fired up the burners while drinks were passed around, and many toasts were made. Some of the other men helped Zak with the cooking, but mostly, it was the Cajun chef who cooked the special—uncharacteristically non-spicy meal—for the newly mated, and newly healed, white wolf.

"To the start of our own little wolf Pack!" Brody raised his glass, grinning at his own toast.

The rest of the guys joined in the laughter, including Marilee and her mother. Their two resident werewolves.

"I thought you built this town for bears?" Laura teased John, who had already accepted her apology for her earlier uncontrollable behavior.

"I did," he confirmed, nodding sagely. "I guess the others who've shown up realized what a good thing we had going here and wanted to join in the fun."

Laura knew it was much more than that. Each new resident had been checked out before they'd been invited to stay. Based on some of the stories Gus had told her about their military days, she imagined every resident of the town had a dossier somewhere in John's office or, perhaps, some even more secure location.

She didn't mind that, really. She was glad to know that everyone here was safe. Living in an area of the world so much more densely populated than what she had grown up with was tough for Laura. She'd already experienced the downside of not knowing everyone in the area. Her first foray to the southern parts of Canada, where a lot more people lived in big cities, had proven disastrous.

The fact that Grizzly Cove was a small town where everybody knew everybody else felt a lot more secure to her. Especially when she factored in the skills that the core group brought with them. They would make sure Grizzly Cove stayed safe for all its inhabitants. They were all protectors, to one degree or another. According to Gus, there were intelligence specialists, terrorism and guerrilla warfare experts, martial arts masters, sharpshooters and snipers, underwater demolition specialists, and a host of other skills represented by the men who had gathered around the Alpha bear.

And, of course, with the addition of the mer in the cove, a whole new set of skills had been added to the town. The few humans who had been let in had certainly made their mark already. As had the alliances with people like the Master vampire of Seattle and the Lords of all were in North America. Little by little, Grizzly Cove was putting itself on the map, so to speak, where magic and shapeshifters, among others, were concerned.

Laura figured she was in good company. The bears weren't quite like a wolf Pack, but they were protective of each other in a way that she found utterly charming. She had her daughter back in her life, and now, she had finally, after a long and circuitous path, found her one, true mate. She had it all, really. Which was pretty amazing considering that, for so many years, she had believed she had lost everything.

Laura could never have predicted the amazing future she now considered. The Mother of All had smiled on her, and Gus had done everything in his power to make it happen. If she hadn't loved him already, that would have been the clincher.

Gus was a warrior of the spirit. Like his ex-military comrades, he fought on the side of Light, but his weapons were of the heart and soul. She could hardly believe she had been so blessed as to find not only her daughter, but the love of her lifetime, all right here in Grizzly Cove.

The swinging doors to the kitchen opened, and for a few moments, everyone's attention was on Zak and his helpers, as they brought out trays and trays of food. He had cooked for an army, she realized, in a somewhat literal sense. She smiled at her own thoughts, and Gus came in for a quick peck on the lips before drawing back.

"What was that little smile for?" he asked in a voice that carried only to her while everybody else was preoccupied with the arrival of the food.

"Just thinking about how lucky I am," she told him, reaching upward to return the tiny kiss.

"Luck was just a little part of it," he told her. "I recognize the hand of the divine when I see it, and believe me, the Mother of All played a large part in recent events."

"I believe you're right." She turned to put her arms around his neck. His arms came around her waist as if they belonged there. And, she realized, they did. Now and forevermore. It was a heady feeling to know that she would have Gus in her life for as long as they both lived. "And I couldn't be more thankful for all the blessings bestowed on me. I never thought I would ever be happy again. I hate to admit to the despondency and lack of faith that plagued me for many years."

"That's all over now," Gus told her. "I won't say it's all going to be blue skies and rainbows from here on out. There will undoubtedly be rain on occasion." He chuckled, and his eyes glinted with humor. "In fact, given our location in the Pacific Northwest, there's probably going to be *a lot* of rain." Laura joined in his laughter, but then, he got serious again. "But we'll weather any storm that comes at us. Together. Forever. You and me, and all our friends. We're a big family here, in case you hadn't figured that out yet. We look out for each other. I won't promise you it will be anything like a werewolf Pack. We don't really go for all that hierarchy stuff—at least not very seriously—but the care and concern are real. The love is real. I know you and Marilee need that closeness of Pack, and we'll try to be that for you. We're bears, but we'll be your Pack."

Laura was speechless for a moment, touched beyond words. That he would worry about something like that only confirmed what she already knew. Gus was *the* spiritual warrior for his bear Clan. He looked after all the souls in Grizzly Cove, including her and her daughter, now.

Laura reached up and stroked her fingers through his hair, holding his gaze, hoping he could see the love in her eyes. "I'm not much of a Pack animal anymore," she told him. "But I believe I could do really well in a Clan." She coaxed his head downward so their lips were only inches apart. "Of course, I'll do well anywhere...as long as I'm with you."

She kissed him then, and didn't even mind the cheering, stomping and loud whistles that started up a minute later. The bears were better than Pack. They were family. The family of those who had fought together, bled together and helped each other through thick and thin.

Gus picked her up and whirled her around, and Laura knew that the moment was perfect. The first of many, she prayed...with her true mate.

EPILOGUE

The next day, Laura met Marilee for lunch at their usual picnic table near the beach. Laura had thought long and hard about whether or not to tell Marilee her suspicions about Roger. Marilee had to know something wasn't right with the supposed mating, but Laura didn't want to hurt her daughter by talking about the bad suspicions she had about Marilee's father. He was still her dad, even if he'd been doing as Laura now suspected, and had coerced her into the relationship.

Marilee brought the lunch from the bakery. Once it was all set out and they'd exchanged a few pleasantries and had a few bites of their bakery sandwiches, Marilee spoke before Laura could pluck up the courage.

"I just want you to know that I'm truly happy for you and Gus," Marilee said, her tone serious, her expression laced with care and love. "I guess my father wasn't a true mate, then?"

Luara shook her head. "I don't think so," she replied carefully. "It was all so long ago, and I was very young. I'm not sure if what I felt then was real, but with Gus, there's no doubt. He's the real thing." Laura blushed a little at her own admission. It was all still very new, and the joy in her heart took her by surprise every time she thought of her true mate.

"Like I said, I'm really happy for you. I know what being with your true mate feels like now, and I'm glad you have that," Marilee told her mother. "You deserve all good things after everything you've been through. And Gus is a great guy. I think I'll like having him for a step-dad."

"Oh, my." Laura blinked. "I hadn't really thought of that."

Marilee giggled. "Don't worry. Gus did. He already told me that he expects me to get him a card for Father's Day."

"When did he do that?" Laura demanded, amused at her mate's antics. She loved the silly bear so very much.

"This morning, when he swung by the bakery on his way out to the res. He brought the elders a fresh batch of honey buns and told me to behave." Marilee laughed outright. "He was in a fine mood. Joking and laughing with everyone. The other customers were teasing him, too, about how they knew exactly what had put him in such a state. The comments got a little dirty from there, but all the other guys waiting for their orders uniformly offered their heartfelt congratulations. Everybody seemed happy to see Gus mated so well."

Laura laughed with her daughter as they kept eating their lunch and chatting. When they were about finished, Laura put her hand over Marilee's and caught her eye.

"I'm really glad you're okay with me and Gus being mated. I love you, Lee Lee, and I always will."

Marilee covered her mother's hand with her free hand and squeezed lightly. "I love you, too, Mama. I'm glad you're happy, and here with me. I've missed you."

Both of them were sniffling and smiling at the same time. "I missed you too, baby, but that's over now, and we have beautiful, new, happy lives in front of us. With our true mates. The Mother of All has been very kind."

"Ain't that the truth," Marilee replied quietly.

*

A few days later, the White Wolf Gallery officially opened for business. It was the first of the galleries in Spirit Bear House to open, but definitely not the last. Laura had worked on the place a little at a time, while also enjoying spending time with her new mate. Together, they'd put the finishing touches on the gallery in time for the grand opening.

Everybody in town gathered to officially open the building for business. Gus provided a barbeque around back, on the beach behind the building, for all his friends and neighbors. He was finally getting to throw that party he'd dreamed about where he provided the feast for his friends. They'd all done so much for him and Laura. This was just one small way he could show his appreciation.

The mer were there in force, mingling with the bears of Grizzly Cove, really for the first time, socially, in any real numbers. That was thanks mostly to Laura and her budding friendship with Francis, who had followed Nansee's suggestion to start working in one of the mer galleries at the rear of Spirit Bear House. Laura had been going over to the two mer-run shops almost every day to help them prepare for their grand openings and had made quite a few friends among the women who were running those businesses.

They had all come out to the grand opening of White Wolf Gallery to show their support for Laura and Gus, and they'd stayed for the barbeque, mixing with the townsfolk more easily than Gus would have expected. A few of the mermaids even paired off with some of the single bears, sitting together down the beach a ways, having impromptu picnics as they got to know each other better.

Laura's murals had been a big hit. Her scrimshaw pieces and the smaller canvases had been remarked upon by almost everyone, and quite a few requests for her to paint murals in people's homes or businesses had been coming in all day. Gus was so proud of her. She'd come such a long way in such a short time. He would do all in his power to see that she kept on thriving here in Grizzly Cove for the rest of their lives.

#

ABOUT THE AUTHOR

Bianca D'Arc has run a laboratory, climbed the corporate ladder in the shark-infested streets of lower Manhattan, studied and taught martial arts, and earned the right to put a whole bunch of letters after her name, but she's always enjoyed writing more than any of her other pursuits. She grew up and still lives on Long Island, where she keeps busy with an extensive garden, several aquariums full of very demanding fish, and writing her favorite genres of paranormal, fantasy and sci-fi romance.

Bianca loves to hear from readers and can be reached through Twitter (@BiancaDArc), Facebook (BiancaDArcAuthor) or through the various links on her website.

WELCOME TO THE D'ARC SIDE...
WWW.BIANCADARC.COM

OTHER BOOKS BY BIANCA D'ARC

Guardians of the Dark
Half Past Dead
Once Bitten, Twice Dead
A Darker Shade of Dead
The Beast Within
Dead Alert

Gifts of the Ancients
Warrior's Heart

Dragon Knights
Daughters of the Dragon
Maiden Flight*
Border Lair
The Ice Dragon**
Prince of Spies***

Novellas
The Dragon Healer
Master at Arms
Wings of Change

Sons of Draconia
FireDrake
Dragon Storm
Keeper of the Flame
Hidden Dragons

The Sea Captain's Daughter
Book 1: Sea Dragon
Book 2: Dragon Fire
Book 3: Dragon Mates

The Captain's Dragon

Resonance Mates
Hara's Legacy**
Davin's Quest
Jaci's Experiment
Grady's Awakening
Harry's Sacrifice

StarLords
Hidden Talent
Talent For Trouble
Shy Talent

Jit'Suku Chronicles
Arcana
King of Swords
King of Cups
King of Clubs
King of Stars
End of the Line
Diva

Sons of Amber
Angel in the Badlands
Master of Her Heart

In the Stars
The Cyborg Next Door

StarLords
Hidden Talent
Talent For Trouble
Shy Talent

* RT Book Reviews Awards Nominee
** EPPIE Award Winner
*** CAPA Award Winner

Welcome to Grizzly Cove, where bear shifters can be who they are - if the creatures of the deep will just leave them be. Wild magic, unexpected allies, a conflagration of sorcery and shifter magic the likes of which has not been seen in centuries... That's what awaits the peaceful town of Grizzly Cove. That, and love. Lots and lots of love.

This series begins with...

All About the Bear
Welcome to Grizzly Cove, where the sheriff has more than the peace to protect. The proprietor of the new bakery in town is clueless about the dual nature of her nearest neighbors, but not for long. It'll be up to Sheriff Brody to clue her in and convince her to stay calm—and in his bed—for the next fifty years or so.

Mating Dance
Tom, Grizzly Cove's only lawyer, is also a badass grizzly bear, but he's met his match in Ashley, the woman he just can't get out of his mind. She's got a dark secret, that only he knows. When ugliness from her past tracks her to her new home, can Tom protect the woman he is fast coming to believe is his mate?

Night Shift
Sheriff's Deputy Zak is one of the few black bear shifters in a colony of grizzlies. When his job takes him into closer proximity to the lovely Tina, though, he finds he can't resist her. Could it be he's finally found his mate? And when adversity strikes, will she turn to him, or run into the night? Zak will do all he can to make sure she chooses him.

Phoenix Rising

Lance is inexplicably drawn to the sun and doesn't understand why. Tina is a witch who remembers him from their high school days. She'd had a crush on the quiet boy who had an air of magic about him. Reunited by Fate, she wonders if she could be the one to ground him and make him want to stay even after the fire within him claims his soul...if only their love can be strong enough.

Phoenix and the Wolf

Diana is drawn to the sun and dreams of flying, but her elderly grandmother needs her feet firmly on the ground. When Diana's old clunker breaks down in front of a high-end car lot, she seeks help and finds herself ensnared by the sexy werewolf mechanic who runs the repair shop. Stone makes her want to forget all her responsibilities and take a walk on the wild side...with him.

Phoenix and the Dragon

He's a dragon shapeshifter in search of others like himself. She's a newly transformed phoenix shifter with a lot to learn and bad guys on her trail. Together, they will go on a dazzling adventure into the unknown, and fight against evil folk intent on subduing her immense power and using it for their own ends. They will face untold danger and find love that will last a lifetime.

Lone Wolf

Josh is a werewolf who suddenly has extra, unexpected and totally untrained powers. He's not happy about it - or about the evil jackasses who keep attacking him, trying to steal his magic. Forced to seek help, Josh is sent to an unexpected ally for training.

Deena is a priestess with more than her share of magical power and a unique ability that has made her a target. She welcomes Josh, seeing a kindred soul in the lone werewolf. She knows she can help him... if they can survive their enemies long enough.

Snow Magic

Evie has been a lone wolf since the disappearance of her mate, Sir Rayburne, a fey knight from another realm. Left all alone with a young son to raise, Evie has become stronger than she ever was. But now her son is grown and suddenly Ray is back.

Ray never meant to leave Evie all those years ago but he's been caught in a magical trap, slowly being drained of magic all this time. Freed at last, he whisks Evie to the only place he knows in the mortal realm where they were happy and safe—the rustic cabin in the midst of a North Dakota winter where they had been newlyweds. He's used the last of his magic to get there and until he recovers a bit, they're stuck in the middle of nowhere with a blizzard coming and bad guys on their trail.

Can they pick up where they left off and rekindle the magic between them, or has it been extinguished forever?

Midnight Kiss

Margo is a werewolf on a mission...with a disruptively handsome mage named Gabe. She can't figure out where Gabe fits in the pecking order, but it doesn't seem to matter to the attraction driving her wild. Gabe knows he's going to have to prove himself in order to win Margo's heart. He wants her for his mate, but can she give her heart to a mage? And will their dangerous quest get in the way?

The Jaguar Tycoon

Mark may be the larger-than-life billionaire Alpha of the secretive Jaguar Clan, but he's a pussycat when it comes to the one women destined to be his mate. Shelly is an up-and-coming architect trying to drum up business at an elite dinner party at which Mark is the guest of honor. When shots ring out, the hunt for the gunman brings Mark into Shelly's path and their lives will never be the same.

The Jaguar Bodyguard

Sworn to protect his Clan, Nick heads to Hollywood to keep an eye on a rising star who has seen a little too much for her own good. Unexpectedly fame has made a circus of Sal's life, but when decapitated squirrels show up on her doorstep, she knows she needs professional help. Nick embeds himself in her security squad to keep an eye on her as sparks fly and passions rise between them. Can he keep her safe and prevent her from revealing what she knows?

The Jaguar's Secret Baby

Hank has never forgotten the wild woman with whom he spent one memorable night. He's dreamed of her for years now, but has never been back to the small airport in Texas owned and run by her werewolf Pack. Tracy was left with a delicious memory of her night in Hank's arms, and a beautiful baby girl who is the light of her life. She chose not to tell Hank about his daughter, but when he finally returns and he discovers the daughter he's never known, he'll do all he can to set things right.

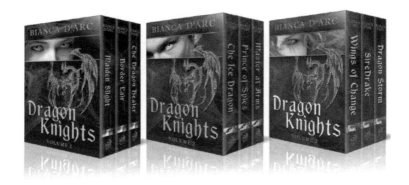

Dragon Knights

Two dragons, two knights, and one woman to complete their circle. That's the recipe for happiness in the land of fighting dragons. But there are a few special dragons that are more. They are the ruling family and they are half-dragon and half-human, able to change at will from one form to another.

Books in this series have won the EPPIE Award for Best Erotic Romance in the Fantasy/Paranormal category, and have been nominated for *RT Book Reviews Magazine* Reviewers Choice Awards among other honors.

WWW.BIANCADARC.COM

60214477R00121

Made in the USA
Middletown, DE
14 August 2019